BAD BLOOD

VOLUME ONE
THOMAS LEES

IAIN McLAUGHLIN

First published in 2015 by Thebes Publishing
Follow us online:
www.thebespublishing.com
https://www.facebook.com/ThebesPublishing
https://twitter.com/ThebesNews
ISBN-13: 978-1-910868-11-9

THEBES PUBLISHING

BAD BLOOD

BAD BLOOD

VOLUME ONE
THOMAS LEES

BAD BLOOD
CREATED BY IAIN McLAUGHLIN AND
DANIEL McGACHEY

BAD BLOOD

'Of all the creatures that walk or crawl or swim or fly only one was not created by God. The vampire alone was borne of Satan and is cursed to live without the blessing of the Lord.'

Brother Merrick de Carnac

France, 1189 AD

BAD BLOOD

Chapter One

They call me Billy Boy.

It's not my name.

My real name... no, it's been given away. To fights over nothing, to nights spent sleeping in the open under a newspaper, to too many bottles of cheap booze I'd either stolen or begged for. My name was given away, and I don't know if I want it back.

I'm scared it's going to hurt.

The name has memories attached. Really bad memories. Baggage I don't want to deal with. Things I'm not able to deal with. It's better to just think about now.

Or maybe better to think about nothing.

I'm in an alley. I'm not sure where. It's been raining – it's been raining all day. I'm wet and I'm cold. That deep cold that doesn't leave you even when day comes. But I think I've been cold for a long time now. I can't remember being warm. Not even when it's sunny. The cars on the street outside the alley are splashing through puddles and throwing up spray. It's that sort of sibilant, hissing wet sound. Like a living thing.

It's warmer in the alley. Steam is coming from vents in the ground and from open windows. I can smell food through the windows as well. Restaurants must back onto the alley. The smell makes me realise how hungry I am. No, not hungry. Starving. I haven't eaten in days.

And then I catch my reflection in a window. I'm a wino. No, that's not me. I know it's not me. But I'm looking at my reflection. I'm old. Under a battered Homberg hat, my hair is long and grey. It's slicked to my head by the rain. I have a beard too. It's matted with dirt. I can see my clothes – they're torn and filthy. My coat and shirt are both worn and ripped and I can feel the rain seeping inside onto my skin.

I'm a wino.

But how can I be a wino? It doesn't make sense. I recognise the smells coming from the restaurant. I can smell boeuf bourguignon, steak tartare... and the bottles in the garbage container. French wines. I know which regions in France they come from. I know how much they cost. I can read the labels – I speak French. So I'm educated. I'm educated and I'm used to living well. How did I come to be this wreck of a human being? Oh, God. I'm rummaging through a restaurant's garbage can, looking for scraps to eat. A rat's beaten me to it. There are half a dozen meals mixed together. They've been scraped together onto a plate before being thrown out. I don't care. It's food. I don't even care that the rat's scuffling about in the food. I chase it away and start eating. Salmon. And it's not just any salmon – it's imported from Scotland. I know this restaurant. Somewhere in my mind, I know all of this.

And then I remember. Not everything. Just enough. More than enough. I was a bank manager – William Edgars. That's my name. I managed the First Texan Bank here in Dallas – I'm in Dallas! – and I was married. I was married for a long time. Emma. My beautiful Emma. Long blonde hair and blue eyes that sparkled with life. A smile that brought sun on a rainy day. We had two daughters, Veronica and Aria. Named after Emma's favourite aunt and my love of opera. They looked just like their mother and we were happy. We had everything we could want.

I had everything a man should ever want.

I was in my office at the bank when the police came. There had been a drunk driver, they said. He'd lost control and hit into the side of their car. It had been quick and they hadn't felt anything. The police were kind about it. There's no easy way to tell someone that everything they've ever lived for is gone. I didn't go to the hospital or the morgue. I just walked out of the office and kept walking. I never went home. There was nothing for me there. I slept that first night on the streets. How long has it been now? Six years? Seven years? Longer? It's hard to keep track. Can I count the winters? It doesn't matter. William Edgars is gone. They call me Billy Boy now. Dear Christ, I had a breakdown and I can't recognise it. I should get help. Get my life back. Wait. This isn't me.

It isn't me.

There's a horrible squeal deeper into the alley, in the shadows. The rat I shooed away. The sound of eating. The same kind of eating as me – frenzied, urgent.

I call out. 'Who's there?' My voice is frail. No answer. I tell them to find their own place, that this is mine. I grab a wine bottle and wave it at the shadows, ready to defend my feed. Then there is a laugh. It hardly sounds human. Thin and pained. It scares me. Most things scare me now, but this is different. I know I'm not getting out of this. And then there's a movement – so quick I can barely see that something's coming at me before it slams me back against the wall. It's a man. He's strong. I can't move. I'm struggling as hard as I can but I can't break free. His arm is across my chest pinning me to the wall. He's dressed in black. I can smell him even over my own unwashed stench. He smells of must and decay. I'm begging him to let me go. He leans forward, bringing his face into what little light the street lamps give. Even in this murk I can see that he is death. His skin is pasty white and flaking off and around the eyes and lips it's lined and shriveled. The lips themselves are black. What little hair he has is long, white and straggling. He looks like some kind of evil scarecrow. I keep begging him to let me go. I'm pleading with him, but I know I'm going to die. He's enjoying the show, watching my pathetic struggle because he knows it's futile. He knows I'm not going to escape. His eyes are dark and hidden in shadows but they're almost glowing with sadistic pleasure. He's going to kill me.

'Don't struggle.' His voice is a whisper but it sounds like broken glass. 'Life has been a struggle for you,' he's saying. 'Let the struggle end.'

And then he smiles. His teeth are all wrong. The front four on both top and bottom and sharp and pointed, like canine teeth narrowing to needle points. Bits of furs and entrails hung between the teeth – from the rat? Oh, Christ, he's eaten the rat. I feel sick at the thought. And then he moves again. I don't even know what he's doing till I feel the teeth tear into my neck and throat. There's so much pain. I try to scream but I can't breathe. There's a gurgling sound. Somewhere in my mind I realise that it's blood coming from my throat. He laughing. He's laughing at what he's done to me. He pulls back. My blood covers his face. Bits of my skin are caught in his teeth. He's on me again. Biting like an animal. My knees are buckling and he pushes me hard to the wet ground. His mouth is at my throat, close to my ear. Before everything fades away, I can hear him. He's drinking. Drinking my blood. Drinking my life.

I'm dying.

The sad thing is the sense of relief that it's all over.

I woke up. Suddenly, like I had been slapped awake.

I was at home in my own bed. The sheets were soaked with sweat and tangled round me so tightly you'd think somebody had tried to strangle me with them. It took a few minutes to get myself free and settled. I looked at the clock. Ten to two. I tried to relax but I knew I wasn't going to sleep again that night. I was too scared that I'd have another nightmare.

No. they're not nightmares.

They're more than just bad dreams. They're much more than that. I wondered if maybe the reason I was staying awake was to stretch as far as I could the time I had before I needed to go to work because I knew what would be waiting for me when I got to the pathology lab. I knew Billy Boy was going to be waiting for me.

I knew he was real.

They had been every other time.

BAD BLOOD

Chapter Two

I was late for work that morning. The damndest thing about not sleeping properly is that you wind up grabbing what sleep you can – even if it's just a few minutes – and you often wind up dozing past your alarm call. That was what happened to me again that morning. I missed the alarm and wound up having the quickest shower in history. I kind of ran in and ran out, hardly giving the water a chance to get me wet. I finally arrived just fifteen minutes late after skipping breakfast and driving too fast. At least working for the cops would spare me a speeding ticket.

As soon as I turned into the parking lot, it was clear something had happened. I hoped I was wrong about what it was.

Reporters and TV crews were outside the building, buzzing like flies round shit. Kind of appropriate. I've never met a journalist I didn't think was an ass-hole. Maybe it's because I only ever meet the ones who come here to the morgue chasing a story, leeching their living from the dead and their families. I doubted that this lot would change my opinion of the journalistic profession much.

A couple of cops were on the door, keeping the press out. Tony Ricardo and Rob Morris. They're good guys. Smart, pleasant, both mad-rabid Cowboys fans and quick to give you grief if you're not – but they're good cops. They deserve better than the graveyard shift. Well, that's what they call standing guard at the mortuary. I guess they must have pissed off somebody high up sometime.

I pushed my way through the reporters towards the door. A couple of them recognised me and started shouting questions.

'Doctor Lees, will you be doing the autopsy?', 'Doctor Lees, do you have any idea why he was killed this way?', 'Do you have any comment, Doctor Lees?'. Yeah, I had a comment but I kept it to myself. The last thing I needed was Victoria seeing me on TV swearing at a reporter.

Tony and Rob finally rescued me, clearing the last few reporters away and shoving me into the building. I thanked them but they were already back to business, keeping the press at bay. Like I say, they're good guys.

I'd been in my office for less than two minutes when Bob Booth showed up. He's slipping. Five years ago he'd have broken the minute. Saying that, five years ago I wasn't head of forensic pathology and he'd have been barging into somebody else's office. I kind of wished it was still somebody else's office. I was tired and just not in the mood for him. He's not a bad kind of guy – just a bit heavy on bureaucracy and paper-pushing for my liking.

'Tom, you're late,' he said. Nice greeting, first thing in the morning.

'Only ten minutes or so,' I answered. 'What's with the circus outside?'

'Another Ripper killing,' Bob said, perching himself on the edge of my desk. 'And this one's on our patch. We're doing the autopsy.' He grimaced a little. 'Well, when I say we...'

'You mean me,' I finished for him. 'What are you talking about? What Ripper?'

Booth looked at me, horrified, like I was some kind of moron. The worst kind of moron. 'Don't you ever read the papers?' he asked.

I shrugged. 'Only Garfield and the sports.'

As a sparkling, witty rejoinder it crashed and burned. Bob tossed a paper onto my desk. 'Here,' he said. 'Read.'

I picked up the paper and resisted checking the sports section first. Bob was pretty agitated. That wasn't good. He was too much of a stuffed shirt to get worked up over nothing. I'm not being cruel. He's my friend and he happily admits to being the most stuffed shirt in Texas. I flipped the paper over. *The Dallas Courier*. Usually a pretty conservative kind of paper but this morning's issue had its front cover given over totally to the latest Ripper killing. A gaudy, banner headline, taking up half of the front page screamed DRAC THE RIPPER. Underneath was a smaller headline, LATEST VAMPIRE-STYLE MURDER IN DALLAS, and beside it was a picture of Christopher Lee as Dracula from one of those English horror films. I looked up at Bob. 'You're kidding.'

He shook his head. 'Read on.'

There wasn't much reason for me to carry on reading. I already knew the details of the murder. It was the murder I'd seen as a nightmare the night before. No, it hadn't been a nightmare – I'd lived through it. I'd experienced it. I could have filled in a dozen gaps for the police. Either that or have been carted off to the nearest nut-house.

'I wish I was joking about this,' Booth was saying. 'Incidentally, you look like something the cat was too classy to drag in.'

'Thanks,' I answered. 'Rough night. Didn't sleep well.' And wasn't that the truth? Best to turn the conversation back to work. 'So what's the score with this Ripper?'

Bob stood up and pulled the door open – it's not a big office. 'Let's get you scrubbed first,' he said. 'I'll explain it on the way.' I followed Bob out of the office and we headed for the autopsy room. 'The psycho is a serial killer who's been trailing across the South for months now.'

'Serial killer?'

Bob nodded. 'An artistic one. He rips out his victims' throats and drinks their blood. He does the whole Dracula bit. There's always extreme blood loss. The Cops think he actually drinks the blood.' Bob looked at me, like he expected me to be shocked, like he wanted me to be shocked. That's just how some people are with news. They love the buzz of seeing the surprise when they pass it on.

I had to disappoint Bob.

How could I be shocked when I'd lived through half a dozen of the killings?

'A psycho with a vampire fetish,' I said. 'Nice.' We were almost at the door to the scrub room attached to the autopsy room. Two black-suited men stood stiffly to attention at the door. They might as well have had big neon signs spelling FBI over their heads. I asked, 'What's with the suits? Feds?'

'There's one more thing about this sicko that the public and the press hasn't been made privvy to,' Bob muttered quietly, as if he didn't want the agents on the door to catch him telling me about it. 'You don't tell anybody about this,' Bob hissed at me. 'Not even Victoria, assuming she ever speaks to you again.'

I grimaced but agreed. 'Setting aside my private life, what is it?'

'Within twenty four hours of each killing our boy comes back for a souvenir.'

That was new to me. In all of my dreams, visions, nightmares… whatever you call them, I'd never seen anything about the killer coming back. But maybe that wasn't surprising when I thought about it – when the victim died, so did my vision. 'What kind of souvenir?' I asked.

Bob looked round again. You'd have thought he was slipping me state secrets or something. 'He cuts off their heads,' Bob whispered. 'Eight times so far. Your autopsy will tell us if this John Doe is number nine. Frankly, I'd say it's a certainty it is but they need you to confirm or deny it..'

'I'll get to it.'

'Great. But keep your ID on show all the time, huh?' Bob tilted his head towards the FBI waxworks outside the scrub room. 'The Feds are a bit edgy about this case.'

I nodded. 'Got it.' And then more in hope that Bob would tell me something other than I thought I already knew, I asked, 'What time did the murder happen?'

'Between half past one and ten after two,' Bob answered. I had to stop myself from slumping. I'd been desperate to hear that it had been four o'clock or quarter past seven. But I'd known it was round about two o'clock. I'd been there, remember?

Bob was still talking. He hadn't noticed my reaction. 'In the alleyway behind deSalvos. You know that restaurant I'm always saying you should take Victoria to.'

'A meal at a fancy restaurant isn't going to get Victoria and me back together,' I snorted.

A grimace worked its way over Bob's face. 'You know your problem, Tom? You're too cheap.'

'Only because my boss doesn't pay me enough,' I snapped back.

'You remembered I'm your boss?' Bob threw his hands in the air melodramatically. 'I must go make a note in my diary.' The suddenly he was serious again, all business. He's like that. It's as though he can throw a switch and go from laughing and joking to deadly serious in a heartbeat. 'As your boss, I'm telling you to get to work,' he said. 'And as your friend, I'm telling you, you really look like hell.'

'You're no oil painting yourself.'

Bob shrugged again and went back to his office. He was right. The worst thing was that I knew he was right. No matter how hard I tried to ignore them or dismiss them, I knew these nightmares were affecting me. But I kept pushing them to the back of my mind. If I didn't think about them, they couldn't be real, right? I'm a doctor. I should know better. Denial's a dangerous thing. Maybe I was denying that I was in denial?

I headed for the scrub room. The two FBI agents standing at the door hadn't moved in all the time I'd been talking with

BAD BLOOD

Bob. I flipped my ID in their direction as I passed. 'Hi. I'm Thomas Lees. Bob Booth said you'd be expecting me.'

They didn't react. It wasn't that they blanked me or anything. They just didn't react in any way. I thought they were being real pros, but something in the way the stood so still wasn't right. I tried talking to them again. 'You were expecting me, right?' Still nothing. I waved a hand in front of the Fed closest to me. Nothing. Even when I snapped my fingers he just stared straight ahead. It clicked what was wrong. They weren't blinking. I guessed they'd been drugged. I tried shaking one. All I succeeded in doing was toppling him into his partner and sending them both onto the floor.

I turned to call for help but I caught a movement through the corner of my eye. Through the glass panel on the door I saw that the door from the scrub room to the autopsy room was open. Somebody was moving inside the autopsy room. If I called for help, I'd send them running. They'd be long gone by the time help arrived. I took the gun from one of the Fed's shoulder holsters. It was heavy, the kind with a magazine in a squared off handle. I'd handled this kind of gun before. Technically I work for the police department so I have to go do a certain amount of shooting practice every month. I know how to handle a gun. I just hate the things. But I didn't see much of an alternative, so I took the gun and eased the scrub room's door open. Moving as quietly as I could I crept over to the door leading to the autopsy room. It was open; there were two people inside. Billy Boy was on the autopsy table, stripped off and ready for me to start work. Even in the fleeting moment I saw him, I could see that his body was painfully thin and covered with livid bruises. Standing over him was a young woman. Most of her face was hidden by long dark hair. I wasn't paying much attention to her face anyway. In one hand she had a long, broad-bladed knife – a machete more than anything. In the other she had Billy Boy's severed head.

20

My hands were shaking but I raised the gun and tried to hold a steady aim. 'Stop right there.' My voice wavered some, but not as badly as I'd expected. Put the knife and the head down.' She began to turn towards me. 'Slowly!' I said. 'I don't know what you did to the Feds out there but don't try anything. I may not be a cop but even I can't miss from here.'

She looked at me – straight at me. She looked like she was twenty or twenty-two, something like that. Twenty-five tops. Not much more than a kid, however old she was. She was around five foot six and slim; she was wearing black. Black boots, black pants, black shirt and black jacket. She wasn't wearing make-up and her dark brown hair hung long with a bit of a wave in it.. Her mouth was probably a little too wide and her nose too snub, but she was a beautiful young woman. But that's not what I saw in her eyes. Her eyes were old, like they'd seen more than anyone should have to see. I'll tell you something else. She wasn't scared. I had a gun pointed at her heart but she wasn't fazed. I wasn't even an annoyance to her. 'Put the gun down,' she said softly. Her voice was smooth and strong but had no accent at all. Odd that a voice should sound strange for not having an accent. 'I don't have time to waste here.'

'Just stand still. Don't move.' I forced myself to keep the gun aimed at her. She didn't move. She didn't blink. She just stared at me. I tried to turn away, but I couldn't make myself move at all. I knew I wasn't moving and I could see that she was standing still, but we seemed to be moving closer together. Slowly, then faster. I couldn't control it. I couldn't stop. I couldn't even call out. I just kept moving until I felt that I was being drawn into her eyes until they were all I could see and then the darkness of those deep brown eyes closed around me.

'Tom? TOM!'

I blinked. It hurt like hell. My eyes were dry and it felt like they were being rubbed with sandpaper when I moved them. They must have been open and staring like the Feds in the corridor.

'Tom?' Bob Booth was peering at me. It took a few seconds to bring the room into focus and to register what was going on around me. A bunch of suits – more Feds probably – were around the autopsy room, examining Billy Boy's headless corpse, one of them was unpacking a fingerprint kit. They were wasting their time. She wouldn't leave anything for them to find.

I tried to move but my legs were woozy and I started to keel over. Bob caught me and pretty much shoved me into a chair. 'It'll take a few minutes to pull yourself together,' Bob said. 'That's if the two Feds on the door are anything to go by.' He snapped his fingers at Louisa, his secretary. 'Gimme the bottle.' I flinched and tried to pull back as Bob squirted cold liquid from the bottle into my eyes.

'Relax,' he growled. 'Don't be such a damn baby. It's only saline.'

I blinked the saline around my eyes and the salt water slowly eased the pain in my head. 'Did you get her?' It was a stupid question. I already knew that she hadn't been caught.

'She?' Bob puffed out his cheeks. 'Who do you mean.' He stopped as he made sense of my words. 'The Ripper's a woman?' He looked back quickly at the FBI agents. 'That's gonna play hell with our FBI friends here. Their profilers never came up with a woman.'

'Well, she was here,' I told him, pouring water from a dispenser into a paper cup.

Bob shrugged. 'Well, maybe that's why she was able to slip away. Nobody was looking for a woman. What did she look like?'

At least that was easy to answer. I'm not likely to ever forget this girl. 'About five foot six, slim, dark hair – long, past her shoulders. Kind of wavy.'

'That it? The FBI will want more than that.'

'She looked kind of European,' I went on. 'And she spoke without any kind of accent. Not American, not English. Nothing.'

'Phony accent?'

'No.' She hadn't been faking the voice. I was sure of that. 'Just completely neutral.'

Bob helped himself to a cup of water and leaned on the shelves next to me. 'The Feds will want to get you together with a sketch artist.' I nodded my agreement. 'They'll want to know why you didn't shoot her. They found a gun in your hand.' He waved a hand in the direction of two dark-suited agents, who were conferring in low voices and sending us filthy looks from time to time. 'Mind you, if they have any questions,' Bob continued. 'I'll be asking how come two of their brightest and best let her pass.'

'I couldn't pull the trigger.' I'd said it without thinking.

There must have been something in my voice. Bob was looking at me in that way he does when he knows something's not right. 'Because you were drugged?' he asked. 'It's the only way she could have knocked you all out.'

There was no way I could have been drugged. She hadn't been close enough and I hadn't been there for long enough – but I didn't want to get into a discussion with Bob. I just wanted out of there. 'Must have been,' I answered.

'Come on. If you're going to answer questions you can do it in your own office.' Bob heaved me to my feet and led me out of the autopsy room. 'I wouldn't be surprised if the first thing they ask is why she didn't kill you or their guys on the door.'

I didn't have an answer for that any more than I could explain why I couldn't shoot her. Or for why I hadn't felt in any danger from her. She'd been there, holding a head she'd just cut off, and holding the blade she'd used to do it, but I'd known that she wasn't going to hurt me in any way. Something in her eyes. Something sad and haunted. It's hard to explain but I was actually feeling sorry for her.

'Shit!' Bob was looking towards the end of the corridor. Three women had come through the main doors. One in her sixties and two in their twenties. The family resemblance was undeniable. Each of the daughters managed to look like her mother without bearing any similarity her sister. I had to stop myself from saying anything. It couldn't be them. It couldn't. They were dead. They'd died in a car crash.

'Our headless boy's family,' Bob muttered.

'I thought they were dead.' It came out as hardly more than a whisper.

'It's tragic,' Bob continued. 'They were in a car smash but the information passed to the cops got garbled. It was the drunk driver and his passengers who died, not these folks.' He sighed. 'But by the time the cops caught their mistake and tried to find him, Edgars was gone. His wife and kids – they haven't seen him in all that time.' Another sigh, this one heavy and from the heart. 'And now I have to tell them that he's had this done to him.' Bob shoved me towards my office. 'Get some rest. You're going to need it.'

Losing someone once was the most painful thing I'd ever been through. I couldn't imagine how it would feel to lose them twice. I wanted to go to Edgars' family with Bob, to tell them how much Edgars had loved them. To let them know, that even when he was broken, Edgars had never stopped loving them. But how could I tell them? How could I tell them how I knew any of that? They'd think I was mad, or worse, playing some kind of sick game. They were going to hurt enough. I... no not me – him, the little bit of Edgars I still felt in my memories – he loved them too much to make them go through that. I closed the office door behind me as I heard someone begin to cry. Aria. She had always been closest to me... *to Edgars*. These were his memories of his family not mine. They listened to opera together. She always cried during *Un Bel Di Vedremo* in *Madame Butterfly*. She would take his death hardest. At least she would have Veronica. She was older, the strong one. She would hold them all together.

I slumped into my chair and tried to push Edgars' thoughts from my mind. They weren't real. They couldn't be. They were just dreams, nothing more. We have our own memories and thoughts, nobody else's.

Whatever else it had done, seeing Edgars' family had forced any thoughts of sympathy for the mystery girl from my head.

BAD BLOOD

Chapter Three

Three weeks after the girl's appearance at the lab, I was getting on with my life.

I had answered all the questions the Feds and the local police had thrown at me, even though they kept asking the same questions over and over. A couple of them were pretty aggressive in their questioning, like I was a criminal. I know it's just a technique but it gets old pretty quick when you're on the receiving end. I've got a short fuse so I gave as good as I got. I won't be getting too many Christmas cards from the people who interviewed me.

I worked with their sketch artists to come up with an image of the girl, which went out to forces and law agencies around the country. I didn't hold much hope for them. They'd only find her if she wanted to be found.

The artist had done a pretty good job. A hell of a lot better than the computer identikit effort. The sketch looked like her – the hair, the nose, the mouth – but not the eyes. What she held in those eyes couldn't be caught on paper. More than once I found myself wondering what had happened to her that she looked so sad.

But for the most part, I'd tried to forget about the whole affair. I had expected the nightmares to torment me afterwards, but none had happened. Not one in all of those three weeks. If my sleep was disturbed at all it was by the girl and her haunted eyes, rather than by dreams of brutal murders.

And so I started to put it behind me. Victoria and I started seeing each other more regularly. It started with a couple of lunches, then dinners and then… and then we were dating. We went to the movies, for meals, even to a couple of parties… we were dating again. It's kind of weird, asking your wife out on a date, but it's exciting as well. I knew that I'd missed Victoria in the year since I'd moved out. I just hadn't realised how much till we started seeing each other again. I was pretty sure she felt the same. I know her well enough to recognise the subtleties in her that show how she's feeling. There's a way she flicks at her hair when she's really happy and dips her chin when she's unsure about asking something. The things you get to know when you live with someone.

Sex wasn't part of the equation yet, which was surprising, I suppose. Whatever else had been wrong with our relationship, the sex had always been great. We were being careful and taking it easy. We had almost thrown away fourteen years because of arguments about nothing. We didn't want to risk fouling up again. We talked about why things had stopped working. We didn't have any definite answers, but we had ideas. We were both 21 when we got married. Too young, according to all of our parents, but we had known better. We loved each other and that was all that mattered. Maybe we *had* been too young after all; perhaps we'd become complacent and stopped working at the relationship. Or maybe we'd become so sure of ourselves that we thought other people would have problems with their marriages but not us. And when the problems did arrive? We just didn't know how to deal with them. Neither of us had enjoyed the year apart, but we weren't going to rush into getting back together either. So we carried on dating. We weren't falling in love again – there had never been any doubt that we loved each other – it was more a case of easing back into each other's lives full-time.

In the three weeks since the girl had escaped from the labs, I'd tried to forget about her. The Feds stopped calling with questions after a while and all I was left with were confused memories and a couple of copies of the artist's sketch. I'd tried to throw the sketch in the trash half a dozen times but I could never bring myself to do it, so it sat on my desk, usually submerged under a pile of paperwork.

That's how it was, late on a Wednesday when Bob Booth stuck his head round my door. 'You still here?' he asked.

I didn't look up from the autopsy report I was reading. 'Nope.'

'Good.' Bob came in and sat on my desk. I hate it when he does that – he usually knocks papers flying. 'You still spend far too much time in this rat-hole.' He caught the edge of a sheet of paper and eased it from the dangerously teetering stack of papers that passed for my In tray. It was the sketch of the mystery girl. 'And you've been spending way too long mooning over this picture, pal. What would Victoria say?'

I was angry with Bob for being so blunt. I hadn't been mooning over the drawing. 'I'm not mooning,' I snapped. 'It's not easy to forget being face to face with a serial killer. And as for what Victoria would say – Victoria and I split up remember?'

If Bob noticed my anger, he didn't let on. 'But you did have dinner with Victoria last night? Spill the beans. How did it go.'

'It was okay,' I answered blandly, still not looking up from the report.

'Okay? Okay isn't an answer. 'Fess up. Did you talk? Did you dance? Did you see a movie? Did you argue? Did you...' He waggled his eyebrows in some weird Groucho Marx impersonation. '...You know?'

I dropped the report onto the desk. When Bob's in that kind of mood, there's no point in trying to work. 'In answer to all of the above, mind your own business.'

'If I had a life, I would. But things are better between you?'

'I think we're getting there,' I nodded.

'So when are you seeing her again?'

'We've nothing planned.' That wasn't strictly true. We had talked about flying to Mexico for the weekend but that was nobody's business except Victoria's and mine. 'We're not rushing things. If we do get back together, we'll do it in our own time.'

'Smart move,' Bob answered, throwing the sketch onto my desk. 'You don't want to screw it up twice. But don't take too much time about it. There are a lot of sharks out there just looking for somebody like Victoria. Now get out of here before I start charging you rent.'

That sounded good to me. It had been a long day. Being honest, they all felt like long days. 'I'm beat anyway. I didn't get to bed till gone one this morning. I think I'll call Victoria when I get home.'

Bob beamed. 'Best idea you've had all day.'

I grabbed my briefcase and the reports from my desk. I didn't even bother putting them in briefcase. 'I'll give these a lookover before bed – if I can be bothered.'

'That's more like the attitude I want from my workers,' Bob said. He planted a hand between my shoulders and pushed me towards the exit. 'Now get lost. And drive carefully in that rain,' he called after me. 'I don't want you winding up on your own slab. The paperwork would be a nightmare.'

I wafted a hand in a loose wave and ran for my car. Calling the rain a downpour wouldn't have been doing it justice. It was more of a monsoon than anything. I turned on the 24 hour radio news station. Turns out we were catching the tail end of Hurricane Winnie, who had faded to a tropical storm as she had swung in across the Gulf of Mexico.

I kept my speed on the sensible side of thirty. The wipers were on full but they were still struggling to give me a clear view of the road ahead. At least most people had shown enough sense to stay off the roads. But even without traffic, I guessed that my drive home would take half an hour longer than usual. Maybe I wouldn't have time to check the reports after all. That suited me. I wasn't in the mood for working. I'd grab something to eat, call Victoria and then grab an early night. The reports would have to wait. I glanced at the soggy pages, sitting on the passenger seat on top of my briefcase. Staring back at me from the top sheet of paper was the girl from the autopsy room. I must have picked up her picture by accident. I flipped the sketch over. Let her look at the reports for a while.

The rain seemed to be getting heavier. No, there was no 'seemed to' about it. The road ahead was getting harder to see and of all things, there seemed to be a mist forming. I thought briefly it might have been condensation on the inside of the windscreen, but the mist was definitely outside. It was becoming damn near impossible to see anything ahead and I was thinking of pulling off the road for a few minutes when the road disappeared. It was still there – I was obviously still driving on it – but that wasn't what I saw through the windscreen. Just for a second, the road was replaced by a dark alley with mist swirling through it. And then? And then it was the road again. I blinked and rubbed at my eyes. I had to be imagining things. I had to be. Bob was right. Too much work. I thought that maybe I should try talking Victoria into stretching our weekend in Mexico to a full week.

And then the road was gone again. Suddenly. No warning, no hint that it was going to happen. I was in the alley. It was the same as when I'd dreamed I was Billy Boy. I knew I wasn't really there in the alley, but somehow I was. I could feel the cold air and mist cutting into me. I could feel the ache of arthritis in my knees and my back slowing my walk to a shuffle. I knew that I was old – an old woman in my seventies. Elise LeVesque. I'd never heard the name before but I knew that was my name and I was in New Orleans. I'd lived there all my life. I'd been living on the streets for the last fourteen years. But that couldn't be. I *knew* that I was Thomas Lees. I *knew* that I was in Dallas driving home through a tropical storm.

But I was also an old woman in New Orleans, looking in an

alley for my cat. My only friend. I can hear some movement in the alley. It's dark. I can't see much. 'Hey, that you, Chico? You found something to eat, cat?' I moved further into the alley. Chico is on the lid of a trash-can. What's left of him anyway. He's been torn apart. Fur ripped open, guts torn out. 'Chico. My poor baby.' I picked up the cat and started to cry. He was the only friend I had. The only one who cared.

I yelled. 'Get out of there!' The part of me that was in the car knew what was going to happen. I screamed at her – at me? – to run, to get out of there, but she stayed there, cradling what was left of her cat.

'My poor baby. Why would they do this to you? Why would they take you away from me? You were all I had.' A movement in the shadows. I knew it was him, the one who had killed Billy Boy. I screamed at her again to run, to get away from the alley. Instead, she turned to face this man who I knew was going to kill her. 'You killed my baby?'

He moved forward, a shuffle more like an animal than a man. His pale skin was a jaundiced yellow in the distant street-light and laughed, showing those rows of rat's teeth. 'Yes.'

And then he exploded forward towards me – towards the woman in the alley. I felt his teeth tear her throat out, cutting off her terrified scream.

In the car I screamed. I could still feel her pain, even as the alley faded and the road became visible again. I was weaving wildly across the road, the steering wheel was slipping through my hands. I tried to control the car, but I was disoriented, dizzy. I couldn't control it. The rain was suddenly heavier again.

It was turning red.

The rain had turned red and oozed thickly down the windscreen, clogging the wipers until they couldn't move. It wasn't rain – it was blood.

It was raining blood.

I lost the back of the car and yanked the wheel to compensate.

It was too late. The car slewed across the lane. It skidded off the road and down an embankment. I vaguely saw the tree ahead and felt the car crash into it hard before I blacked out.

BAD BLOOD

Chapter Four

It wasn't like waking up. That drift into consciousness. It felt like I had to fight my way there. Fight my way through the waves of blackness that kept trying to pull me back to nothingness; to fight through the pain tearing my head apart. When I did wake up I wished I hadn't bothered. It sounds twee, like a bad line, but *everything* really did hurt. Neck, arms, legs, torso. God, my chest hurt. It must have been where the seatbelt went across me. The shoulder screamed as well when I tried to move. How bad would I have been if I hadn't been wearing the seatbelt? It wasn't worth thinking about. But I wouldn't have been in hospital, that was damn sure.

The lights were low but they still stung my eyes like hell when I opened them. It was like someone was ramming fire into them. I heard a horrible moan of pain and I was surprised when I realised that I was the one who had made the noise.

'Thomas?' Victoria's voice.

Victoria had been dozing in a chair near the bed I was in. She was beside me, holding my hand, stroking my hair. In the low light, with her long dark hair hanging forward, most of Victoria's face was in shadow. I could still see the marks where the tears had run down her cheeks and I hated myself for making her cry. I managed to croak something. It was meant to be an apology. It didn't come out that way.

'It's all right. You're all right.' Victoria was squeezing my hand so tight I thought she was going to break it. I didn't say anything. To be honest, I hurt so much everywhere else, I didn't think another broken bone would make that much difference.

'Where am I?'

'Hospital.' She flicked the hair from my forehead. I heard her fingertips brush against something and guessed I had a plaster of some kind on my forehead. 'You crashed your car. Don't you remember.'

'I guess so.' And it came back to me. A dream. I'd had a dream when I was driving. I must have fallen asleep at the wheel.   A dream. Yeah, right. I knew better than that. I hadn't been that tired, had I? If anything, the rain had kept me more alert than usual. But it had been just like the dreams I'd been having. No, not dreams. Worse than dreams. More intense, more real. I could feel them, remember the smells, the taste. I could feel the teeth, feel my life being drained out of me. My life stolen by... what kind of man was he? I almost hoped that I had just fallen asleep at the wheel. 'I was somewhere else.' The words slipped out without thinking.

Victoria straightened my sheet. She was just looking for something to do. 'I don't understand. What do you mean?'

I shrugged. It hurt like hell. 'I don't know. It felt like I was somewhere... I don't know where... what I was doing...' Explaining to her wouldn't have done any good. She would have thought I was nuts. So I just let it drift. 'It probably just a dream I had when I was unconscious.'

'You're not making sense.' She smiled. It was forced. When you've been with someone as long as we were together you get to know when they're putting on a show. 'The doctor says you have a concussion.'

'He could be right. I feel like... well, I don't know what I feel like but it's not good whatever it is.'

She wrinkled her nose. 'I'd hate to think you were feeling good when you look this bad.'

That made me laugh. It hurt but I didn't mind. 'That's why I married you, Vicki. You're all heart.' I knew how she would react. We both knew that was why I'd done it.

'If you call me Vicki again, you'll wind up in hospital for

more than concussion.' She hated being called Vicki. But this was our game. We were playing it out to relax and get ourselves back on familiar ground. We did it every now and then when we were on a date. A reminder that we were still us. Things were different but we were still the same people and we still did the same things. And maybe we could still be together. No. By then we both knew we should be together.

'Who is this?' Victoria was holding the police artist's drawing of the girl from the autopsy room. It was scrunched and there was dried blood on it. My blood. More of it than I liked to think about.

The cops or paramedics must have brought my gear from the crash.

'Who is she?' Victoria repeated quietly.

'She's…' What could I say? Victoria's face was giving nothing away. What I was going to say mattered to her. You just know things like that when you've been with someone this long. The truth was the only answer. 'I don't know. I only ever saw her once. At the labs about three weeks ago. She's wanted… the FBI want to talk to her about some stuff.'

Victoria pursed her lips. Like she wasn't sure if she had done the right thing by asking about the girl. 'She's the killer the FBI are looking for.'

Even concussed, I knew I hadn't told her that. I hadn't talked about the case with anybody. 'How…?'

She interrupted, 'Bob told me about it. He just left before you woke up.' She spoke quickly. 'Why didn't you tell me about it? The FBI? The girl? We've seen each other half a dozen times or more since it happened. Why didn't you tell me, Tom?' She was pissed. Really pissed. A lot. She was keeping a handle on it but her voice was brittle and she had spoken faster than usual. I recognised the signs.

I didn't know how to explain it but I had to try. Victoria deserved that. And I had to try for myself, too. 'I'm not sure why I didn't mention it. There was something... when she looked at me.' I really didn't know how to explain it. I hadn't been able to explain it to myself. 'I froze. I can't explain more than that. I froze.'

I felt Victoria's hand take mine. Warm. I love the way she stroked the back of my hand with her thumb. 'She's a serial killer and you're not used to handling a gun. You don't have to be ashamed of being scared. Anyone could have frozen in that situation.'

'I don't mean that I was scared.' I sounded annoyed. 'Hell, I *was* scared, of course I was but I've been scared before. I just... physically couldn't make myself move.'

She sat on my bed. I felt her hip pressed against mine through the blanket. She wasn't angry. She was pissed because she was so worried. 'Bob said you had been drugged.'

'Maybe.' I looked at the police drawing, then thought about the girl as she'd been in the autopsy room. Those eyes. 'I just know I had a gun pointed at her and I couldn't fire. I don't think I could ever hurt her.'

The words had just come out. I felt Victoria stiffen beside me. Her thumb stopped moving on the back of my hand. She didn't speak. All I could hear was rain on the window. 'You were attracted to her? Is that why you didn't tell me about her?'

I grimaced and reached for a glass of water by the bed. Victoria got there first and held the glass to my lips. The water was warm but welcome all the same. 'She was attractive enough,' I said. 'But I haven't got the hots for her.'

'I'm glad to hear it.' She said it quietly but she meant it.

'She seemed so sad. No, sad isn't the right word. Just filled with so much regret.'

I felt stupid, frustrated that I couldn't explain it to Victoria or to myself. And I was scared. Scared that that something was happening that I didn't understand. Part of me was convinced I was just going crazy with dreams and hallucinations. Another part of me hoped that I was going crazy because it was a lot safer to think about than the alternative.

Medicine doesn't have all the answers. You won't find a doctor who claims it does. But there was nothing I knew of that could explain the hallucinations and dreams any more than I could find a way to explain how I knew everything about Billy Boy and the others who had been killed. And it wasn't just what I knew... it was what I felt. Billy Boy's love for his family, his despair when they died. I didn't know how to explain away how I felt when I saw them. As for the girl... I hadn't been lying to Victoria. I wasn't attracted to the girl at all. At least not in the physical or sexual way. But there *was* something about her. Not something I could put into words. Just a feeling. Even now I can't explain it. Lying in that bed, I felt stupid for not being able to make myself understand.

Victoria could sense the frustration. She would want answers soon enough but she let it drop. 'This is a hell of a way to get out of a vacation with me in Mexico.'

She had changed the subject and I was grateful for it. 'I'll be there. Even if I have to bring half a dozen hot nurses to look after me.'

She punched my arm softly. 'Try it and you'll be straight back in here, buster.' She caught my hand in both of hers. 'And I'd rather not go through this again, even if you do look cute when you're helpless.'

'Thanks. I still love you. You know that, right?' I hadn't planned that. It just came out. It was true but it just happened.

She smiled. It was that smile she had when was really pleased about something but didn't want it to show. 'Now you tell me. When you're in no condition to do anything about it.'

'There's plenty of room in here beside me.' It was supposed to sound playful. I don't know how it sounded to Victoria. To me it just sounded weak and pathetic.

Victoria's smile was genuine and it seemed to relax her.

'Somehow, I don't think your doctor would approve of my bedside manner if I did that. Besides, you need your rest. If we started fooling around you would have a relapse.'

'Worth it, though.'

Victoria laughed. I had missed seeing her smile. 'Save that thought for when you get out of here.'

'Sounds like a promise to me.'

The smile slipped from Victoria's face. She took a moment before she spoke. 'When you get out of this place, I want you to move in with me for a while.'

'How long is a while?' I asked.

She pursed her lips in a non-committal kind of way. 'We'll see.'

'Is this a spur of the minute thing because I'm in here?'

Victoria's answer was quick and honest. 'No.' She took a breath, as if she was worried I thought her answer had been too fast. 'No. It's something I've been thinking about for a while. A long while.'

'Good.' I wanted to say something more from the heart, more impressive. I didn't know what to say that wouldn't sound wrong so I repeated, 'Good.'

Victoria kissed my forehead. 'We'll talk about this when you get out, okay? For now, I'm going to let you sleep.'

I protested. 'I just slept for God-knows how long.'

I felt her fingers brush hair away from my brow. A pain stabbed through me even when she touched the skin accidentally. I guessed I had hell of a bruise up there. 'Unconscious isn't sleeping.' She kissed me again and left. It's strange to say, given that I was in a hospital, banged up to hell because hallucinated about a storm of blood... but I was happy. Victoria wanted me to move back in. That was all I wanted to think about.

I was happy.

I had started drifting into sleep when I heard the door open. It was Bob Booth. He looked tired. He hadn't shaved. 'So, you're not dead.'

'Sorry to let you down.'

Booth shrugged. 'Just so you know, I'm docking you pay for being asleep when you should be at work.'

'Talk to Victoria about that. She deals with the money.'

'Try to take money from a bank manager?' Booth snorted. 'Even I'm not stupid enough to try that.' With the small talk out of the way, Bob relaxed just a bit. I could see how concerned he was. He was ca good friend.

'What brings you here?'

'Smart ass,' he smiled sourly. 'I just looked in to see if you were okay. You're better than I thought you would be.'

'Better than I have a right to be.'

He didn't disagree. 'I passed what's left of your car earlier. It's going to take more than a couple of nights in hospital to fix that. I don't know how you came through that, Tom. God must really love you.'

'I was thinking more that the Devil loves his own.'

Bob chuckled. There was no real humour in it. More relief. 'Well, your sense of humour is back to normal. And That's not a compliment, by the way.'

He stayed a while longer. We talked about work, about Victoria. He was pleased I was moving back to Victoria. Moving home. He didn't push me about going back to work. He told me to take time and get myself sorted before I thought about work. All through the conversation, there was something I wanted to ask, but I didn't. It would sound crazy. How could I ask about blood on the windshield? Had the rain really been blood? I would sound crazy.

Maybe I was crazy.

Would it hurt to talk with a shrink after I got out?

'Tom?' I blinked. Bob was looking at me. He was concerned, but not in a worried way. More like he was fussing. I must have stopped listening to what he had been saying, too busy in my own thoughts. 'You're tired,' he said. 'I should let you sleep.'

I didn't argue. I *was* tired.

Bob waved a goodnight and tossed his newspaper onto the bed. 'I've read it already. There's no good news but it might pass some time in here.'

After Bob left, I tried to sleep. My body was tired. My brain too. But sleep wouldn't come. I don't know why. A nurse offered me something to knock me out. I asked for a bottle of Jack Daniels. She didn't see the funny side and left. In the end I gave up and accepted that sleep would come when it was good and ready.

I picked up the newspaper Bob had dropped on my bed and lost all interest in sleep.

A huge black headline on the front page.

VAMPIRE KILLER STRIKES AGAIN.

Just underneath, in smaller letters:

NEW VICTIM FOUND IN NEW ORLEANS

There was a picture of a street. I recognised it. The street I had seen when the rain turned to blood and I crashed the car.

I hadn't *seen* it.

I had *been* there.

I had felt the rain. Felt the attack. The death.

Chapter Five

I have to be honest. I don't remember what happened after I saw the newspaper. I know what I did, I just don't actually remember doing it. It felt more like I was just a passenger and things happened without me actually choosing to do them.

I have no memory of getting dressed. There was a cab straight to the airport and a flight to New Orleans. I know I took them but I don't remember any details. Even when I got to New Orleans, it didn't occur to me that I had no luggage. I remember getting in a cab. I don't know why I asked to be taken to the city mortuary but I know that I did. I don't think I had even thought of where I would go after I landed when I was on the plane. But in the cab I had known.

The mortuary's front doors were open and untended and I knew that something was wrong. They had a dead body in a high profile case. I expected to see at least a couple of uniforms on the door. After two sets of swing doors I found one of the FBI agents who had been in Dallas the night I had seen the girl. It took a moment to remember his name.

'Charteris!' He didn't move. 'Charteris?' His eyes were open but not moving, he didn't blink. His body was rigid and stiff. Just like the FBI agents I had seen in Dallas. Just like I had been.

It had to be her.

She was there already.

I shook Charteris. Shook him hard and slapped him. Slapped him again and his eyes started to focus. 'What... happened?' His voice sounded dry and painful. Ignored it.

'Never mind that. Is she here? Did you see her? The girl?'

'Girl?' Charteris's eyes swam. He was trying to pull his

thoughts into order. 'There was a girl. Dark hair.'

'The one your sketch artist drew?'

He nodded. He was like a rag doll. 'I saw her. I told her to stop.'

I knew the rest. It had been exactly the same for me. But she was there and that meant I could get some answers. 'Where are the corpses?' I asked Charteris. 'Where will the victim be?'

'Just here.' He led me round a corner. His legs shook under him. He was like Bambi. A door was slightly ajar. He said, 'That's it, but I should have two men on duty here.'

'Do you have any other men here? Or security?'

'No. There was another murder downtown. I sent my men to investigate, to see if it was our killer's work.'

'No.' I hadn't felt anything since the car crash. No dreams, no hint of anyone else's thoughts or memories. I knew it wasn't the same killer. 'Come on.' I reached for the door.

'Shit.' Charteris's hand hovered near his empty shoulder holster. 'My gun's gone.'

I hadn't thought about weapons anyway. I honestly didn't care. 'It doesn't matter.'

'Are you crazy?'

It was too late. I had already pushed the door open.

She was inside. The girl I had seen in the mortuary back in Dallas. She looked exactly the same. Same clothes, same hair, same expression on her face. That look of sadness.

'Don't move.' Charteris's two missing Feds were inside the room. They were both unconscious on the floor. Charteris had retrieved one of their guns and had it pointed squarely at the girl's heart.

She ignored him. 'You?' She was looking at me. She sounded mildly surprised. She certainly wasn't bothered by the gun pointed at her.

'Shut up!' Charteris snapped. He flicked his pistol in the direction of the machete in the girl's hand. 'So that's what you use, to cut the heads off.'

She still didn't look at Charteris. She was trying to work out what the hell I was doing there.

'Is that true?' I asked.

She didn't answer straight away. As if she was deciding whether or not to waste her time on me. 'Yes,' she said finally. 'The cadavers must be decapitated.' She was totally matter-of-fact. She might as well have been talking about opening a can of food.

'Not this one,' Charteris said. 'Put the blade down.'

She spoke to Charteris but still didn't look at him. He had a gun aimed at her heart and she wasn't even slightly concerned. 'You must let me finish my work.'

Charteris took a step towards her. His grip on the gun was tighter than it should have been. The knuckles were white. 'You call hacking up dead bodies work?' His voice was shaking. 'You're a sick piece of work. Put the blade down.'

She didn't move.

'Put it down!' Charteris's voice was close to cracking. Hell, *he* was close to breaking.

'Keep it calm,' I said softly. 'She can't do anything to hurt us. You've got the gun.' She looked at me in a strange sort of way, then slowly put the machete onto the surgeon's table. She lifted her hand clear so we could see she was unarmed.

Charteris moved alongside me and swiftly slipped the pistol into my hand. 'Keep her covered. I want to see if she's touched the body.' He moved towards the table, keeping a distance between himself and the girl. 'If she moves, shoot her. Aim to kill.' Charteris kept the bed between himself and the girl as he inspected the body. 'We got here in time, The head is intact.'

The girl's hand moved. Not much. Hardly more than a twitch, really, but I caught it. A flicker in the direction of her machete. When she looked at me, she knew I had seen it. Her voice was still calm, neutral. 'Time is short. You must let me finish my work.'

Charteris was still edgy but it was obvious his confidence was coming back. Whatever had happened before didn't matter. He had the situation under control now. 'You're done with your work. You're under arrest for murder and God knows how many other crimes.'

There was another movement. I thought the girl was twitching towards her machete again but it wasn't her. The woman on the table. The woman who had been murdered. Her hand moved. How could it? I had been in her head, felt her die. I could see that her throat had been ripped out. But I would have sworn I saw her hand move.

'What is it?' Charteris had noticed that something had bothered me. I didn't have time to tell him what it was.

The old woman on the slab moved again. This time it was so fast I hardly saw it. Her hand shot up. Faster than I could ever have imagined. Her fingers caught Charteris's throat. He gagged and tried to pull away. Her fingers ripped into the neck, tearing his skin, gouging deeper. She sat up, like she was a third of the age she seemed. She moved fast, dragging Charteris's throat to her mouth. His mouth was open but only to let blood bubble out. There was nothing left in his eyes. She was drinking his blood, sucking it from his open throat.

I pulled myself into some sort of sense. 'Let him go.' I aimed the gun at the old woman. 'Let him go!'

She dropped Charteris. His head made a sick thudding sound as it hit the ground. The old woman was staring at me. Blood covered her face. It was smeared on her cheeks. The bizarre thing I noticed was that the gaping wound on her own neck had healed. It was gone. When she spoke, blood bubbled from her mouth. 'Fresh. Need fresh.' Her top lip curled up in a sneer and I saw her teeth. Long and sharp. Bit of Charteris's neck hung from them. She slipped from the bed, light and easy on her feet. The way she looked at me... I knew she was going to do the same to me she had done to Charteris. And then she was coming at me. Faster than I could believe.

Instinct took over. I was still holding the pistol and I squeezed the trigger. Over and over. I saw the bullets rip into her chest, force her to stagger backwards. I emptied the gun into her.

And she smiled. The bullets hadn't affected her. Her lips peeled back and she was coming at me again. I threw my hands up to protect myself and saw a silver flash in the air. The old woman's face look startled for a second then her head was yanked backwards, clean from her shoulders. The body dropped to the tiles. The girl held the bag lady's severed head in one hand, her machete in the other. She stuffed the head into a rucksack she had put against the door. I hadn't noticed it before. The way she handled the head she might as well have been stowing a towel after a work-out at the gym.

'What happened?' It was a stupid question, I suppose. I just couldn't make my brain accept what I had seen.

'What did you see?' she asked.

'I saw you cut that old woman's head off.'

'Then that is what happened.' She reached for the machete. I hadn't even noticed that she had put it down to stowe the old woman's head. I lifted the gun instinctively. It didn't faze her at all. 'It's empty.' She glanced at the clock on the wall and then strode the few steps to Charteris's body. She lifted him by the hair. Blood was still dripping from what was left of his neck. She dropped him face down across the table. She pulled the machete back, ready to swing. She was going to take Charteris's head as well. I reached out to catch her arm but she spun, so fast I barely saw it. She caught my wrist like I was a kid. I couldn't move it. How could she be so strong?

'You're crushing my wrist.'

She pushed me away. 'You have hindered me enough today. I have no more time to waste with you.' And she swung the machete again, straight through Charteris's neck.

'For God's sake, why are you doing this?'

She stopped. When she looked at me, there was something different about her manner. Something... not gentler, but less bullish for sure. 'I am doing this for God's sake,' she said.

'So what are you? A religious nut? Some religious serial killer?'

She grabbed for a sheet. 'Why do so many people with no faith assume those with faith are insane? Who gave you the right to be so arrogant?' There was real anger in her voice.

'Then tell me who you are. Why the hell are you doing this? Are you the killer Charteris was chasing?'

She wrapped the sheet around Charteris's head. She was noticeably gentler with his head than she had been with the bag lady's. 'You don't believe anything you have seen tonight, do you?'

'I don't believe anything that's happened to me in the last couple of months.'

That piqued her interest. She hid it but there was a flicker in her eyes. She pushed it away. 'Good. That will make it easier for you to forget everything you have seen here.'

'That's not going to happen.' I was sure of that. 'Unless you've got another Jedi mind trick to play on me. Or unless you're going to kill me.'

'I'm not going to kill you,' she said. 'I will tell you the truth. You will not believe a word I say but I will tell you. I am not the killer your friend was seeking. He is still out in the city somewhere and he will kill again and again until I stop him.'

'Are you government?' Charteris - what was left of him - was still slumped across the table. 'You're not a Fed. Charteris would have known.'

'No, I work for a...' she paused, a little sneer of distaste flitting across her face. '... a different organisation. A much older one. And before you ask, no, I will not tell you its name.' She took a step towards me and looked me straight in the eye.

'But I will tell you this. My name is Rebecca, and I must find this killer because he is a vampire, one of the oldest and most powerful, and I must find him before he takes another victim.'

She believed it. There was certainty in those sad brown eyes. She really believed every word she was saying. 'A *vampire*? Come on, vampires don't exist. They're like ghosts. Boogeymen we tell our kids about.'

'You saw one rise with your own eyes and still you do not believe.' Her voice was angry and dark with contempt. 'Is your mind so closed that you cannot accept what you see for yourself?'

Words tumbled out of me. All the shit I had kept bottled up. The dam burst and they poured out. I couldn't have stopped even if I had wanted to. 'I don't know what to believe. For months, I haven't known what was real or what was a dream. I don't want to believe the things I see in my mind are real but I saw her... the bag lady...'

It hit me hard, like an explosion in my brain. I felt like I was on fire, burning from the inside out. I screamed and felt my knees buckle.

The girl caught me. 'What is wrong?'

'I don't... I...' She was blurred, fading. I could see something past her. A street, wet with fine rain.

'Concentrate.' The girl's voice was sharp, cutting through the pain. 'Tell me what is happening.'

I felt like my skull was splitting but I had to answer her. I knew I did. 'The killings,' I managed to gasp out. 'I see these killings in my mind. I feel them. I live them.'

'You have the sight.' She sounded far away but I could make her out clearly.

'I don't know what that means.' I could feel the rain now. The fine rain that covers you and coats you, it gets through your clothes, through to your bones so you can't feel dry or warm for hours. The street was mostly dark. A lot of the street lights were out. Broken. Some of the shops were boarded over. Others had writing in their windows. In French. When I tried to focus on anything, the pain ripped through me again. 'Get it out of my head. Leave me alone.'

'No.' Her hands dug into my arms and I clung to that physical pain. It kept me in the real world. My world. She was still talking. 'You must open your mind. Let it was over you.'

'I can't.'

She shook me. Hard. 'you must.'

'It's tearing my mind apart.

Her voice was calm, like the pain in my arms from her grip, it was something to hold on to. 'If I can stop him from killing, then your visions may also stop. Do you understand?'

I choked out a sort of yes.

'Tell me where you are,' she went on. 'Tell me what you see around you. Even a small detail will help.'

'Definitely here. This city.' I didn't have to see any details. I knew I was in New Orleans. I just felt it. Same way that I felt the cold and the hunger. 'The French quarter. A run-down street. There's no-one around but me.'

'How can you tell?'

'I just know.' Who else would be out in this kind of neighborhood so late at night? It was dangerous. I had been beaten by a drunk not far from there a few days ago. No, not me. *Him*. I felt the pain from his broken ribs.

'I need to know exactly where you are. Focus on one thing. What do you see in front of you? Relax your mind. Tell me what you see.'

I tried to do what she said. If it made the dreams stop I would try anything. I relaxed my mind, let the images come in. It hit me harder than before. I felt disoriented, dizzy, like I was going to puke. But I could focus. I could see. Details were clearer. 'I see a shop. A small one. A baker, I think. There are pastries and bread in the window. God, I'm hungry. I'm thinking about smashing the window to steal them.'

'What is the bakery called?'

I focused on the letters. Forced them to become words. No, one single word. 'Cantonvilles. It's called Cantonvilles. I need that bread. It's days since I ate.'

'Do you know your name?'

'I'm...' The answer started to come but I couldn't put it into words. It was like a memory, something I knew but couldn't bring to the front of my mind. I closed my eyes to concentrate but it wouldn't come. When I opened my eyes, they refocused. Not on the name 'Cantonvilles' elegantly stencilled on the window in flaking paint, but on the face staring back at me. A wreck of a man. Long, dirty hair, a matted beard, an overcoat that hadn't been clean since I stole it from a drunk in a doorway. It was the face that stared back that shook me. Painfully thin with dull, unhealthy skin and sunken eyes with dark bags under them. There was no life in the face. A man who had given up on life and who was waiting for death. I knew why. His memories were bleeding into me. The broken marriage, the drugs, kids with petrol and a book of matches. How could anyone have done that to me? Not me, him. I had to remember, it wasn't me. It was him. The poor bastard. 'I'm a vagrant,' I said. My voice felt lifeless, dull. 'I live on the streets.'

'How can you tell?'

'My reflection in the shop window. I see myself. I don't care how I look. I don't care about anything.' A sound. Something on the wet pavement. Something moving fast.

I slammed into the wall. I didn't have time to register the impact in my side before I was hitting the wall, hard. I can't move my arm. I think my shoulder is broken. And then I'm lifted. Like a toy. I can see my reflection in the shop window again. I'm floating the air. Twisted but floating. 'Something's got me. It's there.' I could hardly squeeze the words out. The grip around my throat was so tight. Long fingernails digging into my skin.

Rebecca's voice was urgent. 'What do you see?'

'Nothing. It's got no reflection.' I tried to turn my head but I couldn't. The grip was too tight. In the corner of my sight I could see an almost bald head. There were a few thin, brittle hairs on the grey skin. He smelled like rotting meat. I screamed. I saw two holes appear in my neck. I heard a laugh. A vicious laugh. It was all hate. There was another sound, like an animal feeding and then all I could feel was pain as I watched the reflection of my throat being ripped open. It was biting. Savage. In a frenzy. 'Tearing my neck open.' I tried to choke words out. To tell Rebecca what was happening. 'It's feeding on me. I can't move.' Abruptly, the pain stopped. 'It doesn't hurt now.' The words came more easily.

'How do you feel now?' Rebecca asked.

There was a contentment settling on me. Acceptance. Was I glad to be dying? Was death better than living on the streets? 'Sort of pleasure.' No, that wasn't right. 'It's more like… joy.'

And then I was falling to the ground. I didn't feel the impact though the sound told me my skull had fractured. Looking up I saw him. A skeleton with dead, grey skin stretched over it. His teeth were pointed and sharp. My blood was smeared all over his face. And that laugh on his face as he watched me die. There was madness all over his sick face.

I was relieved when I died and it all went dark.

I don't know how long it took me to come round, to be myself again. In my own head. When I did I realised I was crumpled on the floor. Rebecca was cradling my head. For the first time, she showed some hint of emotion.

'I think I'm losing my mind.'

'You are not insane,' she said quietly. 'But you are psychic.'

I tried to sit up. 'Bullshit.' I was still too shaky to think about standing up. 'I'm a doctor. That psychic stuff is…'

She cut me off. 'You *are* psychic. Whether it is a gift or a curse for you, I do not know. However it is exactly what you are.' Those eyes. She pinned me with them. 'And in your heart, you know it is true.'

I didn't believe her. Didn't want to believe her. Just the word psychic brought up images of those bullshit TV shows with fakes giving their gullible marks phony messages from their dead ones. It was show business and exploitation. Preying on grief for money. It was sick.

But this wasn't fake. I still felt it. The pain of my throat being ripped out. The pain of my living a dead life on the streets. It was real. And I knew Rebecca was telling the truth. 'Fuck.'

'Can you stand?' she asked. I gave it a try. I was shaky but I got there. 'Good. We have little time.'

'Where are we going?'

She swung the bag holding the bag lady's head onto her shoulder then picked up Charteris's head. 'You told me where the next victim is. We need to get to him before anyone else finds him.'

'Why not phone the police? Let them handle it?'

A sour expression flicked over her face as if I had disappointed her. 'Because the police as as sceptical as you. They will take the body to the morgue and when he rises again in two days I will be hunting two vampires instead of one. That is why I have to find him first.' She started to leave then stopped at the door. 'You have been useful. Are you coming with me?'

It was my way out. Just get on a plane, fly back to Dallas, sleep beside Victoria. I could do that. And never know the truth about what happened to me? No, this girl, Rebecca, had a way to stop the visions. I had to stay until it was done.

BAD BLOOD

Chapter Six

We had slipped out of the morgue easily enough. It was late and the few Feds who had been there were still glazed over. Rebecca's hire car was parked in an alley a few minutes' walk away. It was dark and average. Ideal if you didn't want to draw attention to yourself. She put the severed heads in the trunk, then swiped the screen of her cellphone and launched her internet browser. She had an address and direction to Cantonville's in under a minute.

The drive there took fifteen minutes, maybe less. The rain had got heavier and I was grateful. It would make people stay inside. When we pulled up at the bakery, we found the body stuffed into a doorway.. I recognised my face.

His face.

The neck had been ripped out and his eyes were open, staring at us. 'God, what a mess.'

'You are a doctor.' Rebecca sounded surprised. 'I would have thought you were used to blood and open wounds.'

I snorted. 'I'm a pathologist. I cut up dead people to find out why they died. I've seen worse than this. I just didn't enjoy living through his death.'

Rebecca knelt to examine the corpse. 'Unfortunately, I know this vampire's ways too well. I have pursued him for years. I almost caught him in Massachussetts two months ago but he escaped while I dealt with his servant.'

'Years? How old were you when you started chasing this crazy?'

'Young.' She glanced up and down the street, making sure we were still alone. 'What matters is that I do not let him escape again. He is growing bolder, moving from the alleys into the open. Why is he becoming so brazen?' You could see her pushing the thought aside and she looked back at the vagrant's corpse. 'There is nothing we can do for this one other than save him from rising as a vampire.' She produced a small bottle from inside her coat and tipped the contents over the body. Steam and a sick-looking mist rose from the body. Within seconds it rotted and crumbled to dust.

'Holy water?' I asked. She seemed surprised and nodded. 'I've seen a few horror movies. You know, Bela Lugosi, Gary Oldman, Christopher Lee.'

'Forget them,' Rebecca said brusquely. 'They have distorted the truth about vampires. They won't save your life when we find Corsini.'

I'd thought the truth about vampires was that they didn't exist. Hell, I still wasn't convinced. Not the conscious part of my brain anyway. 'You sound pretty sure you'll find him.'

She was swiping her phone again. It looked like it was from the high end of the market. 'He will have found a place to rest, but he will not be there now. If he is going to stay in this city for any time he will remain out and learn his way around the streets.'

'So he could be anywhere in the city?'

Rebecca shook her head. 'I know him. He never strays too far from his lair. We know the locations of his victims...' She had a maps app running on her phone. It must have been tweaked somehow. She had been able to add the locations of the attacks. 'That narrows the search area considerably. The first attack was some distance from here so we should begin our search somewhere in the middle.' She scrolled the screen and reduced size so she could see more of the city. A few city blocks were swiped across the screen before Rebecca stopped. She enlarged the map to show a cross of green land. 'Here.'

It was an old graveyard, the dates on the stones going back to the late eighteenth and early nineteenth centuries. The place smelled musty, old. It smelled of decay. It hadn't seen much care lately. Stones were broken or had fallen and they were all covered with a heavy growth of moss. The weeds were thick and overgrown. It probably hadn't been touched since the levees had burst flooding the city. An old graveyard just wouldn't have been top of anybody's priorities.

Rebecca moved ahead of me. She had a new rucksack over her shoulder and somewhere under her coat, I knew she had a sword. It was short-bladed and Japanese. I'd seen her take it from the trunk of her car. 'It is near here,' she said softly. 'I can feel it.'

That didn't make sense. 'How can a vampire rest on holy ground?' I asked. 'Or is that something the movies got wrong?'

Rebecca stepped over the broken remains of an ancient wall. 'This was a church graveyard. That wall was the churchyard's original boundary. This land beyond it is not holy ground. It has never been consecrated.'

'How can you tell?' I asked. 'Your app tell you that as well?'

She ignored the smart-ass comment. 'Corsini likes to be this close to a church. It gives him a thrill to mock God.'

The graveyard stretched out about a hundred yards or so. There was no moonlight and we were too far away from any street lights for me to see anything. The blackness only got thicker as we moved further into the graveyard and I started to feel cold. Really cold. It was nothing to do with the rain.

Rebecca seemed to see better in the darkness that I did. 'Here,' she said quietly after we had been walking for about a minute.

I could just about make out a large stone crypt, roughly the size of a room. Rebecca put her hand on the wall of the crypt. 'He has been here.' She pushed a couple of objects into my hand. 'A crucifix and holy water. Take them. They will be your only protection against him.'

The crucifix felt strange in my hand. Uncomfortable. 'Look,' I said. 'I don't know about a crucifix. I don't really believe in God.'

I heard her shrug and her silhouette slipped inside the crypt. 'Then you are lucky that he seems to believe in you. Follow me. Be careful and be quiet.'

It was dryer inside than I had expected. For some reason I thought it would be wet with water dripping down the walls. But it was dry. Dry and freezing cold. I felt something underfoot and I almost fell trying to avoid stepping on it.

'Bones,' Rebecca said. 'They must have been inside the coffin when he came here.'

'I can't see a damn thing.'

A thin beam of light flicked on and she handed me a torch. 'Be careful with this. If he sees it, he will run.' I nodded that I understood. I flicked the light across the floor. A skeleton was scattered carelessly across the floor where it had been thrown out of the coffin. I had stepped on a shin when I had come in. 'Turn the light over here. To the coffin.' I did as Rebecca told me. The coffin was old and musty but some of the material inside remained intact. A pouch was set inside the coffin near the middle.

'So vampires really sleep in coffins?'

'Some,' Rebecca answered. 'Not all.' She picked up the pouch and ripped it open. Something dry and rough spilled out. 'But a vampire of his kind must rest on his native soil. Even this much is enough.' She threw the empty pouch into the corner of the crypt. She opened a small bottle, like the one she had given me and tipped holy water into the coffin, covering the inside from one end to the other. White discs, the size of a large coin were placed into the coffin, carefully set out on the shape of the cross. 'He will not find rest here.' She glanced quickly at her watch. 'He will return soon. The sun will rise in less than an hour.'

'And sunlight kills vampires?'

'Another Hollywood myth.' She almost sneered that at me. 'Sunlight is not fatal to vampires, it simply weakens them.'

'But the cross?'

'Your movies were right about that,' she said softly. 'Vampires do fear the cross. More than anything else. Now turn off the light and move as far into the dark as you can.'

I turned the torch off. 'Okay.'

'And if I fail…' she faltered. I hadn't expected that from her. 'If I fail you must destroy him.'

'I'm just a doctor. I never killed anybody.'

'Vampires are already dead,' Her voice was quiet but cold. 'You have seen what happens to his victims. We finish him tonight. Do you understand?' She was serious. She was going to stop this Corsini tonight even if it killed her.

'I…'

She cut me short. 'Be quiet. He's coming.'

I pushed myself back into the darkness. She must have been wrong. I couldn't hear anything. Even with my eyes adjusting to the darkness I could see virtually nothing. Just the vague shape of the crypt door. I had almost stopped breathing, taking shallow sips of air through an open mouth just to be quieter. After a few minutes I was sure she was wrong.

And then I heard a sound. Fingernails slowly dragged along the crypt's wooden door. I was sweating, the hairs on the back of my neck went rigid. I hoped I had imagined it. Hoped it wasn't real. Then I saw the shape of the door change. Something was coming inside. When it spoke, I knew the voice from my dreams. I knew him. He had killed me so many times.

'Rebecca.' He sounded pleased. 'I know you are here. I recognise your stench.'

I heard Rebecca move on the far side of the crypt. Her footsteps were careful, measured. I could make out her shape in the dark. A little light seemed to be coming through the crypt's door. Dawn couldn't have been far away. 'Count Corsini.' Her voice was calm, even. 'Or may I call you Gregori? I have waited a long time to see you again.'

The light was definitely improving as dawn came closer. Murky grey light came through the door. I caught a glimpse of Corsini's awful face as he stepped from the light into the shadows. He and Rebecca were circling the coffin, keeping it between them. 'I have looked forward to see you again.' That brittle voice in the darkness terrified me. It could have been coming from anywhere.

Rebecca's eyes seemed better adjusted to the dark than mine. Her eyes stayed fixed on a point in the blackness. 'If you do not mind me saying, the years have not been kind to you. You were so handsome once.' She was taunting him, trying to force him to make a move. I didn't miss that her hand was close to the front of her jacket, close to the hilt of her sword.

Again that voice came from everywhere in the darkness. 'You can expect no mercy from me. For everything you have done to me. For the years you have plagued me, for killing Collins... I will make you beg at my feet.'

Metal caught the dull light as Rebecca slid her sword from under her coat. 'I don't think so.'

'You would take my head?' I didn't hear him move. I just felt the impact as he slammed into my chest, crushing the air from me. 'In front of a human?'

'I gasped for air. He had me crushed against the wall. His face was so close I could see the teeth. I could smell the decay from him. I'd been through this before. It was exactly like I'd lived through in the dreams. He was going to kill me, exactly the same as he had done before.

'Get the hell away from me!' I struggled, pushed at him. Swung my fist into his face and caught him flush on the jaw. He didn't flinch.

'You have spirit. The blood of those who relish life tastes so much sweeter than the filth I have lived on.'

His hands gripped my face. The fingernails dug into the skin. I tried to shake him off, to break free. I hit him again and again. He didn't move.

'Let him go.' Rebecca was only a few steps away, her sword was raised, ready to swing at Corsini.

He wrenched me round, holding me between himself and Rebecca, using me as a shield. 'Swing, Rebecca. Take my head. But if you do you will kill your friend.'

'You know better than that. I have no friends.' She meant it. And she was right. We weren't friends. But she didn't make a move.

'Then swing the blade.' He knew she wouldn't do it. He knew she wouldn't kill me to get at him. He knew *her*. They had some history. 'You have no spine for this battle,' he sounded disgusted by her. 'You never had any fight in you.'

He swung me round till I felt the backs of my legs hit the side of the coffin. I couldn't break free no matter how hard I struggled. 'This one has fight, he will enjoy the chase, the euphoria that comes with taking the blood.'

'Kill him,' I screamed. 'For Christ's sake, kill him.'

Rebecca still didn't move. 'Will he enjoy sleeping in a coffin, Gregori?' she asked blandly, and then she added, with real venom, 'Can you sleep in your coffin?'

His head flicked to the side and he saw the cross of communion wafers in his coffin. He let loose a wail like an animal in agony. He threw me aside and turned to Rebecca. She was already flying over the coffin at him, bringing her sword down. He caught her arm and swung her against the wall. She smashed into the stone, hard. It didn't slow her. She lashed out, kicking Corsini in the gut, knocking him backwards. She was on him again, kicking and punching. She had been trained. Trained well. Every blow was precise and hard and she fought with a brutal rage. She hated Corsini. Even in the dull pre-dawn

I could see the hate in her face as she attacked him again and again, forcing him backwards, knocking the coffin from the stone dais it had rested on. The coffin splintered but they ignored it. She kept attacking him, hitting him over and over until his back was to the wall. Her fist was flying towards that dead face again when his hand shot out and caught her throat. It was like she had never touched him. He lifted her off the ground. I could hear her choking. 'You underestimate me, Rebecca. I am the oldest of the vampires. You cannot defeat me.'

Her words were barely legible as she fought against his grip. 'I... have... to...'

He slammed her against the wall. Again and again. She kicked at him and drove her fists into his face. He ignored her. The sick bastard started to laugh. As he crashed her repeatedly against the wall, he started to laugh. 'Are you ready to meet that precious God you love so much?'

I looked for the sword but I could see it. There had to be something I could use. What had Rebecca given me? I felt the bottle and the crucifix in my pocket. The coffin was in front of me, smashed. I pulled one of sharpest shards of wood free.

He was still smashing Rebecca into the wall. Still laughing at her. The fight was gone from her. Her head lolled as she hit the wall. He'd probably broken her neck. I rushed at him, shoved the crucifix into his face. He screamed and dropped Rebecca. His dead skin burned where the crucifix touched him. I swung the shard of wood with all my strength, ramming it into his chest. He reeled backwards. The wood was deep in his chest. I drove it deeper with the heel of my hand. Every bit of strength I could find. He looked down at it in surprise. He was shocked at what I'd done.

And then he started to laugh again. He straightened up. It hadn't worked. 'The heart, human. It must be through the heart.' His hands grabbed my arms.

And he screamed.

The flesh on his palms blistered and belched foul-smelling smoke as the skin burned. Holy water. I had tipped the bottle I had been given by Rebecca over myself. If he touched me, he would burn. I shook what was left from the bottle at him. It hit his face and the skin burned and peeled. He tried to circle towards the door looking for an escape.

He screamed again. Another splinter of wood burst through his chest. This time it had come through his back. Rebecca pulled herself to her feet. I was amazed she was alive, let alone standing.

'Through the heart, Gregori.'

Corsini staggered, trying to stay on his feet, his hands clawing at the thick wooden splinter Rebecca had driven through him. She lashed out with a foot, kicking his knee out from under him and he toppled. He struggled to a kneeling position. Rebecca had already scooped up her sword. Blood bubbled from Corsini's mouth as he struggled to speak. 'You don't… have… the courage…'

Rebecca swung hard. The sword sliced through his neck in one stroke. I can't describe the sound it made but I'll never forget it. Corsini's head toppled onto the stone floor. His eyes were wide open, so was his mouth. Blood still oozed from his mouth. Rebecca picked it up and looked at the face for a few moments then threw it outside.

'I can't believe he's finally dead.' It was like someone had cut the strings on a puppet. She slumped back against the stone dais the coffin had been resting on. 'He's really gone.'

I kicked the remains of Corsini's body. 'He's dead all right. I thought you were, too,' I admitted.

She twisted, trying to ease a pain in her back. She suddenly looked tired. Tired and much younger than I had thought. 'I should thank you.'

I didn't know what to say. I shrugged. I didn't want to think

I'd been involved in taking a life. Even this… whatever he had been. I still struggled to accept that vampires were real. 'What do we do now?' I asked.

She stood, and winced as she did. She nudged Corsini's body with her boot. It had started to crumble. 'This will be dust in a few hours.' She picked up her bag and wiped her sword on Corsini's clothes before slipping it back under her coat. 'But it would be best for us to get away from here before the city comes alive.'

Chapter Seven

Outside, the sun still hadn't quite risen but the tell-tale glow was clear low in the sky. Corsini's head lay in the thick grass. Rebecca picked it up. This time she didn't look at the face. She simply carried it to the church wall and threw it onto the other side. Even before it hit the ground, the skin had burst into flames. It turned into an miniature inferno. Within thirty seconds, all that was left were ashes. 'Holy ground,' she explained.

She handed me the car keys and asked me to drive. I asked her if she wanted to go to the hospital. At the very least I was sure she had to have a concussion and her back was obviously giving her a lot of pain. But she refused and directed me through the early morning traffic to a small motel on the edge of town. It was somewhere between low-class and no-class but it was quiet and nobody paid any attention as we pulled up out front and dragged ourselves into the end room.

Inside there were two main rooms. One small living room with a beaten up couch, a TV and a basic kitchen. Through the open door I could see a double bed. Rebecca said another door led to a bathroom. The place looked like it had been decorated in 1975 but I didn't care.

'It's not exactly the Ritz,' Rebecca apologised. She sounded exhausted, dead. Pretty much how I felt.

'Wouldn't know,' I answered. 'I've never been to the Ritz.'

'It's delightful,' she said absently. 'At least it was the last time I was there.' She pointed to the couch. 'You can sleep on that.'

I sank onto the couch and didn't care how lumpy it was. Rebecca returned a few moments later with a couple of blankets. I thanked her and then she was gone, closing the door to the bedroom behind her. I stretched out and dragged the blankets over myself. It suddenly occurred to me that Victoria would be worried, and that I should call her but I didn't have the strength to reach for my cell-phone. I was asleep seconds later.

I don't know how long I slept. I don't know exactly what time we got to the motel, but it was getting dark outside when I was wakened by a noise. The click of the bedroom door opening. Rebecca came through. She was wearing a baggy black t-shirt and black leggings. Her thick, curly hair was tousled. A bad case of bed-head.

'It's you,' I mumbled.

'Were you expecting someone else?'

I rubbed my face and tried to shake the sleep from my head. 'It just took me a minute to work out where I was.'

'I didn't mean to wake you,' she apologised.

'Don't worry about it,' I answered automatically. 'What time is it anyway?'

She checked her watch. 'After five.'

'Shit. We slept all day.'

She nodded, and her hair bounced making her look younger again. I wondered how old she actually was. 'We had a long night,' she said softly.

'That's one way of describing it.' A long night... and a full day for Victoria to worry herself sick about me. 'Shit, I need to phone Victoria.'

'Victoria?'

'My wife,' I answered. 'She doesn't know I came to New Orleans. I was in hospital. She's going to kill me for this.'

Rebecca nodded her understanding. 'I will take a shower while you call her.'

'Thanks.'

Rebecca stopped at the bathroom door. 'By the way, my name is Rebecca.'

'I know. You told me in the morgue.'

She nodded. 'But I don't know your name.'

'Shit. You don't?'

She shook her head again.

'I'm Tom. Thomas Lees.'

She nodded. 'Hello, Tom. Make your call. Talk with your wife. She will be worried.'

The door closed behind her and I heard the shower start to run. I had switched my phone off when I boarded the plane in Dallas and I hadn't thought to turn it on when I landed in New Orleans. I had seven missed calls and a shitload of messages from Victoria. I didn't read them. I didn't need to. I knew exactly how worried she would be and I was going to get enough guilt when I spoke with her.

Victoria answered on the fourth ring. She didn't let me speak. 'Tom? Are you all right? Where the hell are you? What happened?' She kept hitting me with questions.

'Victoria. Victoria.' I damn near had to shout her name to her stop. 'Victoria, it's ok. I'm ok.'

'Where the hell are you?' I knew from her voice that there were tears now. I wasn't sure if they were anger or relief. Or both. 'Why did you leave the hospital?' She took a breath. 'Tell me where you are. I'll come get you.'

'I'm not in Dallas,' I answered. 'There was a...' Shit. How could I explain what had happened? 'There was a case I had to help with,' I said. 'A murder.'

'The serial killer,' she said flatly. I supposed it must have been all over the news by then.

'I can't say,' I answered. It was evasive and I was avoiding the truth, but I needed time to work out what to say to her. What I could tell her that she would believe. 'I don't know what I *can* tell you but I'll tell you as much as I can when I get home.'

'When?' she demanded. 'When will you be home, Tom?'

It was late enough that I doubted if I would get a flight that night. Besides, I still needed some answers from Rebecca. 'Probably tomorrow,' I answered.

'Not probably.' There was no arguing with that tone. I knew her too well. She wasn't asking. This was an order. 'I want you home tomorrow. I don't care who you piss off and I don't care who dragged you into this. You're not a cop, you're not Quincy. I want you home safe.'

'Tomorrow,' I agreed. 'I promise.'

'You'd better be here.' She was shaking. I could hear it in her.

'I'll call you when I book my flight,' I promised.

She didn't answer straight away. 'You're sure you're ok?' she said finally.

I didn't feel ok, that was for sure. I hurt all over. From the crash and from the fight with Corsini and just from being exhausted. 'Tired,' I admitted. 'A few cuts and bruises but I'm in one piece.'

'What cuts and bruises? What happened?'

'I'll explain tomorrow,' I promised. The shower had stopped. Rebecca would be out of the bathroom any time. I didn't want Victoria hearing anything to give her the wrong idea... or anything that would leave me explaining more than I wanted to. 'I've got to go. I'll call you tomorrow.'

'Okay.' She didn't want to finish the call.

I wished I didn't have to. But I knew I did. The bathroom door clicked open. 'I love you,' I said into the phone.

The answer was quick. 'I love you back.'

'Bye.'

'Bye.'

I hit the button to kill the call and looked up at Rebecca. She was wearing black jeans and a black blouse. It had some loose ruffles at the front and the cuffs. Her hair was damp and the curls looked looser and longer. 'I'm done,' I said.

'She nodded. 'I did not mean to interrupt.'

I shrugged. 'No problem.' Jesus, it even hurt to shrug.

Rebecca flipped the switch to turn the main lights on. She was moving easily. However badly she had been hurt the night before, she was hiding it well. She moved easily. 'You should shower,' she said. 'And then we should talk.'

'You think?' That sounded more smart-ass than I had intended but she wasn't offended. I looked at myself in a wall mirror. Those few cuts and bruises I had mentioned to Victoria looked a hell of a lot worse than I had imagined. 'I'm a mess.'

'You'll live.' Rebecca's voice was closer than I had expected and I turned sharply. She was standing behind me, peering at my reflection in the mirror.

It took a second to realise what was wrong. I must have done the dumbest double-take in history as I tried to work it out. She moved away towards the couch, but it finally clicked.

Rebecca hadn't been in the mirror behind me. She didn't have a reflection.

'I'm sorry,' she said, calmly folding my blankets. 'That was foolish of me.'

'You're one of them.' I could hardly speak. 'You're one of them. Aren't you?' I scrambled across to where I had discarded my jacket and fumbled in the pocket for the crucifix. 'You're a vampire.'

Rebecca put the blankets onto the couch. 'Yes.' She was matter-of-fact about it. 'I am a vampire. I will not hurt you.'

I found the crucifix and held it out in front of me. 'Damn right you won't.'

She wasn't afraid. The crucifix didn't scare her at all. She just walked towards me calmly.

'Keep away from me.' I pushed the crucifix towards her again.

She stared at me. Those sad eyes. I remembered movies where vampires had hypnotised people. Was that what she had done to me? To the FBI agents? She wasn't hypnotising me now. She wasn't trying. She reached out slowly and took the crucifix from my hand. It didn't burn her the way it had blistered Corsini. She handled it reverently, lifting it to her lips, kissing the feet of the Christ on the cross. She held the crucifix out to me. 'It was me who gave this to you, remember?'

She was right. I didn't take the cross from her. I wanted space.

'I will not hurt you,' she repeated calmly. 'You have nothing to fear from me.'

'You expect me to believe you? After what I saw last night?'

She was thoughtful for a moment. 'Probably not,' she admitted. She reached into a bad and produced a pointed wooden spike. She pressed it against her chest, pushing the sharp edge hard over her heart. 'Take the end of the stake,' she said.

'Don't be stupid.'

Her hand moved fast as a rattlesnake, catching my wrist until pulling it till my hand rested on the blunt und of the stake. 'If you do not trust me, all you have to do is push. You have seen what happens when a vampire is staked through the heart.'

I struggled to pull my hand free. 'I'm a doctor. I don't kill people.'

She just pressed the stake harder against her chest and smiled a little. A rueful half grin. 'You can't kill me, Thomas. I'm already dead.'

I tore my hand free. 'I'm not going to kill you.'

She left the stake in place for a second, then dropped it back into the bag. 'I am... relieved to hear that. I have a great deal to do.' She picked up her coat. 'I assume you are hungry? You can ask me questions while you eat.'

We drove to a diner on the edge of town. It was almost

empty. I wondered how a place like that could stay open. A bored middle aged waitress glanced at us as we entered than went back to watching a game show on TV. We took the booth furthest away from the door. I didn't say anything.

'You have questions?' Rebecca asked finally.

No shit? 'What are you?' It came out harsh and accusing. I didn't care. I was more confused than ever, and now I was scared as hell of this person I had thought I could trust.

'You know what I am,' she answered, glancing quickly to make sure the waitresses were out of earshot.

'Then why didn't the cross burn you? Why did it burn Corsini and not you?'

Another glance at the waitress. Satisfied that the woman was still lost in the gameshow, Rebecca spoke. 'Most vampires fear the cross more than anything else. With most, it is your best defence. But a few of us, just a few of us, held our faith after we were turned vampire. We have learned to control the bloodlust and the passions the others give in to. Our faith in God has saved us.'

'God?' I was going to say something then stopped myself. Telling a vampire who kept herself in check only by faith that I thought that faith was a load of superstitious rubbish didn't seem like my best idea.

She carried on. 'We devote our years to tracking down out own kind. If we cannot save them from their base instincts, we save their souls.'

'By taking their heads?'

Her eyebrow lifted a little. 'Would you prefer we let them run free? The world would be overrun in a year.'

I didn't have an answer for that. One vampire had caused chaos. What would more do? 'How many of you - of them,' I corrected myself. 'How many are there?'

'Nobody knows exactly how many vampires exist. Most hide in the shadows, covering their actions. They will destroy their

own victims rather than leave any trace of their actions.'
Rebecca stopped as her phone beeped. She hadn't bothered
personalising her ringtones. 'A text message,' she explained,
and read the message quickly.

'Vampires with cell-phones. They never show that in the
movies.'

She glanced up from the screen. 'How do you imagine we
communicate? Trained bats with messages tied to their legs?'

I shrugged. 'I thought it would be something more mystical.'

She slipped the phone back into her pocket. 'Years ago, we
left messages in the advertisements sections of newspapers. We
make use of whatever is available to us. Now we use text
messages if something is important.'

'Was that important.'

She didn't answer straight away. She was sizing up whet she
should tell me. How much I needed to know. 'I have to go back
to London,' she said finally. 'One of my colleagues has
discovered something unusual.' She straightened up at the
waitress shuffled over. The game show had gone to commercial
break.

'What can I get you?' she asked.

I ordered burger and fries with coffee. I didn't expect
Rebecca to order but she did.

'Steak, please.'

'How d'you like it, hon?' the waitress asked automatically.

'Very rare,' Rebecca answered.

'How rare is that?' the waitress asked.

'Raw,' Rebecca answered blandly.

The waitress was going to say something, but I cut across her.
'She's pregnant.'

The waitress - her name tag read Sandy - nodded sagely.
'With me it was peanut butter. Don't worry, hon. It's a phase.
It'll pass.' And she was gone, passing the order in to the chef
and back staring at the TV before her game show started again.

Rebecca cottoned on to my surprise at her order. 'I can eat small amounts of most food but I need raw meat several times each week for nutrition and...' She stopped, embarrassed. 'And it keeps thoughts of blood at bay.'

It was obvious she didn't like to admit that she had the same aggressive urges as other vampires. Knowing she could have that bloodlust wasn't making me particularly comfortable either. What if she had lost control while I was asleep? She could have ripped my neck out and there would have been nothing I could do to stop her.

But she hadn't. She hadn't threatened me at all. In fact, she had protected me. I changed the subject. She deserved a break. 'So, you're heading back to London.'

'The message was intriguing. I will fly there tomorrow.' She didn't offer anything past intriguing. Our meals arrived quicker than I had expected. When I saw Rebecca's steak I understood why. It wasn't exactly raw but it wasn't far from it. The outside had browned slightly but the inside was still pink. She cut the steak into small pieces and ate delicately and slowly, washing the meat down with a bottle of water. I think part of me had expected her to attack the meat like an animal. She ate a small amount of the accompanying vegetables just for show. I finished before her. I hadn't realised how hungry I was and I had eaten much quicker than I normally would. She pushed the side plate of potatoes in my direction. I didn't turn them down.

Conversation kind of dried up while we were eating. Eventually, Rebecca asked me about Victoria. I told her everything. How we had met, dating in college, getting married, the good times and then the split, about talking in the hospital about me moving back in. Rebecca didn't comment at all, she just let me talk. She didn't offer anything about herself or any relationships she had. Hell, I didn't even know if vampires had relationships.

After a while I became aware that Rebecca was glancing

regularly at the shiny chrome metal plate on one of the diner's internal doors.

'You're watching that door a lot. Are you expecting trouble from in there?'

'No.' She sipped at her water. 'But it is time to go.'

She paid the check and left a good tip. Probably the best Sandy would see all year.

Rebecca walked briskly to the car. She didn't look around. That worried me. She had always been looking around for trouble, even when we left the Motel. If she wasn't keeping her eye peeled for a threat, she had to know one was already there.

She drove on the edge of the speed limit, carefully timing her stops at lights so that we would pull away just before the light changed colour. Anything following would have to jump lights or break the speed limit to keep up with us. I kept my eyes on the wing mirror and didn't see any of that happening back along the street. Rebecca took a left and then a quick right and another left.

'We're being followed?' I asked.

She took the next right. 'I thought we might have been. I'm just making sure we're not.'

Chapter Eight

The drive back to the Motel took three times as long as the trip to the diner had taken but by the time we pulled into the parking lot there was no way anyone was following us.

Rebecca led the way into the motel room. 'Just to be safe, we move hotel tonight.' She stopped dead in front of me. 'Wait.'

The light flicked on. Five men filled the small living room. Four were standing. They were all young, built like pro wrestlers and wore black suits. I would have bet money on them being FBI if it wasn't for the fifth man. He was older, around seventy but he had taken care of himself. He wore a black suit with a plain black sweater. Even though that I could see that he had kept himself in good shape. His beard was gray and trimmed short, like the little rim of hair he still had on his bald head. Age may have taken his hair but it hadn't taken any of his intelligence. Even in a shitty little motel you could see in those blue eyes what a formidable man he was.

Formidable enough to have come from nowhere to be elected pope three years earlier. The first British pope in history. I hadn't paid much attention to his election as Pope Andrew I but I guess if you don't recognise the Pope when you see him, you're not paying enough attention to the news.

'He smiled warmly but didn't rise. 'Rebecca, I'm glad you're still with us.'

'So am I.' It was interesting that her eyes flicked around the Pope's bodyguards rather than at the man himself. She didn't trust them.

If the Pope noticed Rebecca's unease he didn't mention it. He looked at me with interest. 'Have we interrupted something? If you have found yourself a young man, I apologise for disturbing your plans.'

'He is not my lover,' she answered quickly - and almost succeeded in keeping the annoyance out of her voice. 'His name is Thomas Lees. He is a human who helped me with Corsini.'

'Indeed?' Pope Andrew's eyebrows went up in surprise. 'It's unlike Rebecca to accept help, even when she needs it. Thank you, Mr Lees.'

'I can't say it was a pleasure, your... sir... what do I call you?'

I never imagined a pope laughing but this one did. Heartily. 'Officially you should call me Your Holiness, but since I'm not actually here, I won't hold you to it.' He explained, 'According to my staff, I'm in my hotel in Washington, getting over a nasty little cold. It's why I'm missing dinner tonight with several cardinals and bishops. However, I must recover by tomorrow or your president will be offended he doesn't get his public blessing.'

'Why are you here?' Rebecca asked. That annoyance still hadn't gone from her voice.

Pope Andrew smiled at me conspiratorially. 'Rebecca doesn't trust the church these days,' he said. 'And I can't really blame her. She's been fighting for the church and under our protection for almost three centuries, but in that time four popes have ordered her hunted and killed.' He looked straight at Rebecca. 'But she should remember that I am not one of them. I have gone to considerable lengths to ensure that can't happen again.' She didn't meet his eye and his tone softened. 'I'm very fond of you, Rebecca, and I do understand why you don't trust the church. But you should be able to trust me. We have known each other a long time.'

She nodded after a moment. 'I do trust *you*,' she said. 'But not the organisation.'

He didn't seem put out by that. 'It's a start.' He waved a hand at the couch, ushering us to sit. 'You asked why I'm here. Well, there are two reasons. First, if you had failed with Corsini, we would have dealt with him and avenged you.' He smiled. It was genuine and I could see Rebecca relax a little. 'But I'm very glad we don't have to do that.' He reached out and squeezed Rebecca's hand. 'And I'm glad for you that it's finally over.' Then he straightened, all business again. 'But something is happening. They made a discover over in England today.'

'Fisk sent me a text message about it,' Rebecca confirmed. 'I was planning to fly back tomorrow.'

'Before you go, I have some more information. It's not an isolated incident. A warehouse here in New Orleans was set on fire...' he glanced at the nearest of his bodyguards. 'About two hours ago?' The suit nodded. 'It wasn't an accident. My men here did it... after staking four vampires who were using the warehouse.'

That really intrigued Rebecca. *Really* intrigued her a lot. She leaned forward on the couch. 'But they never gather in numbers like that. It's safer for them to stay alone.'

'I know,' the Pope agreed. 'But we have word of them gathering in Bucharest, in St Petersburg, in Nice... London, as Fisk will show you when you get there.'

'Why are they gathering?' Rebecca asked. 'I've never known them do that. I've watched them for centuries. It must be why Corsini came to New Orleans.'

'Undoubtedly. You were lucky he hadn't met up with the others.'

'So were you,' Rebecca said quietly. 'If he had been there, these men would all be dead.' The bodyguards, or whatever the hell they actually were, didn't take kindly to that but they didn't say anything. 'I doubt if I would have defeated him alone.'

The Pope scrutinised me. 'What's his story?'

'He is psychic,' Rebecca said. The Pope leaned forward, interested. Rebecca continued, 'He was linked to Corsini's victims. He lived through the deaths with each of the recent victims. His visions allowed me to track Corsini far more quickly than I could have otherwise.'

'Then we are lucky to have found you, Mr Lees.' The Pope stood and started pacing. 'And I don't believe in luck. Something big is coming. The vampires are massing, and just when we need him, a man with this rarest gift falls into out laps. That is not luck, Mr Lees. You have been sent to us for a reason.'

'Sent by who?'

Pope Andrew was a bit startled by the question. It passed quick enough. 'By God, of course. He sent to us for whatever is to come.'

'No way.' I shook my head, rejecting the idea. 'I don't believe in God. Not yours, not anybody's.'

He smiled at me. A wry smile. 'Well,' he said. 'It looks like He believes in you. That's why He gave you this gift.'

I didn't like how any of this sounded. Not one word. 'It's not a gift.' I fairly spat the words out. 'I lived through murders. I lived through my own death, time after time. That's not a gift. That's just cruel, a punishment. And she...' I jabbed my finger at Rebecca. 'She told me the dreams would stop after Corsini was dead.'

'They might,' the Pope said thoughtfully. 'Then again, we have no way of knowing. You can discuss it on the flight to London. I want you to accompany Rebecca there.'

'Go to hell.' The words just came out.

And the room went silent.

I had just told the pope to go to hell.

He was surprised. His bodyguards went pretty quickly from surprised to looking like they were going to kill me. Even Rebecca didn't say anything. So I did.

'My life is in Dallas. My wife is there. She's waiting for me. I've put her through enough. Tomorrow I'm getting on a plane but I'm not going to London. I'm going home.'

'We need you.' He was angry and didn't try to hide it. I didn't care. He wasn't the only one who could get angry.

'My wife needs me. I'm not part of your church, I'm not part of any of this. I didn't ask for these visions and now I'm taking Rebecca at her word. She said the dreams would stop and until I know otherwise, I'm believing her.'

'And what will you do when the vampires come? Say they can't attack you because you're not part of this?'

'Don't give me that shit. You can use guilt on you people. Doesn't work on me. I spent thirty five years walking this planet thinking vampires were bad B-movie boogeymen. I'm betting I can spend the next thirty five going back to doing the same.'

He spent the next hour trying to persuade me. I wasn't interested. I just didn't want to know. Those dreams and the encounter with Corsini had wrecked my life. They'd damn near ended my life. I just wanted to go home to Victoria. In the end, he had to head back to Washington. He was damn angry. As he left he asked Victoria to talk sense into me. Outside was the car Rebecca thought had been following us. It had another two of the Pope's musclemen sitting in it.

Rebecca closed the door.

'Well?' I asked. 'Are you going to try to persuade me?'

She picked up the TV remote and turned on the news. 'No,' she said. We watched the local news reporter talk about a sudden warehouse blaze. She turned it off after that item. 'My flight is early tomorrow morning. You should get the earliest flight home, too.'

I agreed. I wanted to be home as soon as I could. With that, Rebecca said goodnight and went to bed. I was relieved she hadn't tried to persuade me. After what we had gone through together, I think she might have made me change my mind. She didn't try and I appreciated that.

All the same, lying on the couch that night, sleep didn't come as readily as it had the night before.

At the airport next morning Rebecca booked my flight. She asked for my phone and put her number into the memory. Just in case I needed anything. We didn't shake hands, there were no hugs of farewell. We just said our goodbyes and went our separate ways.

Chapter Nine

I didn't know what to expect when I got back to Dallas. I'd talked to Victoria a couple of times on the phone from the departures lounge and she'd sounded really pissed with me. I can't blame her. We'd talked about getting back together and I'd run off to New Orleans after some mystery girl. The worst of it was that I couldn't explain it all to Victoria. I didn't believe it myself so how could I expect her to?

'Oh, honey, it's okay. She's not a killer really. She's a vampire hunter, sent by the Vatican – and the real shocker is… she's a vampire herself! Oh, and by the way, I told the Pope to go to hell.'

No. I'd lied to Victoria. I'd told her that Rebecca worked for an agency that tracked this kind of serial killer. It was true to an extent – though I'm sure Rebecca would remind me that there are sins of omission as well. I just hoped that Victoria would eventually forgive me for charging off like that.

I certainly hadn't expected Victoria to be waiting for me when my plane landed. But she was. She didn't smile and her eyes gave nothing away at all. She can hide her emotions better than anyone I know. It was clear that she was making an effort to keep her reaction neutral and then she just grabbed me and hugged me and squeezed me like she was trying to break me.

'Don't ever do that again,' she hissed.

There were tears welling in her eyes but she wasn't going to let them come. She wasn't going to let me see how much she'd been worried.

I didn't have any luggage so we were able to just head straight for the car without waiting at the carousel. Victoria kept her eyes straight ahead as she drove. She wasn't interested in a conversation. I just settled back in my chair and let the dusty scenery sweep by.

After the best part of half an hour – all of it passed in silence – Victoria took a left on Jeffers. 'Where are we going?' I asked. She should have gone straight on then taken a right to get to my apartment.

She didn't answer straight away. She didn't have to. I knew this road well enough. I'd driven it often enough to know it like the back of my hand. A few minutes later she pulled the car into the driveway in front of her house. Our house.

'Home,' she said. She got out of the car and headed for the house. My car was already parked in the driveway. Inside the house, cases were stacked against a wall and boxes, filled with books, ornaments – everything from my apartment – were piled high in the den.

'I didn't have time to unpack,' Victoria said. 'It seemed like a good idea to move you back in while you were away.'

'Victoria,' I began, but she cut me off. She was walking round the room, still wearing her jacket, and she wouldn't look at me.

'You know how useless you are with this sort of thing,' she said quickly. 'You'd only have been in the way, getting under my feet. It's better this way.'

She was talking too fast. You know the way people do when they're desperately angry or upset? I caught her arms and turned her to face me. 'Victoria…'

I didn't see her hand coming up to slap me until an instant before my jaw exploded with burning pain. 'If you ever do anything as stupid as this again I will never forgive you! Do you understand me?' She was crying now, but this wasn't some weak weeping – the tears were coming through anger. She was literally shaking. 'I will not go through that again. You will not put me through that again, you selfish bastard.'

I know what I did was right. I'd had to help Rebecca. It was right. And it was the only way to stop the dreams. But I hadn't thought about how it would affect Victoria. I should have. I should have thought about her before anything else. I shook my head. 'It's done. I don't have to do anything more.'

Victoria sort of nodded. It was still more like she was trying to stop herself from shaking than a genuine nod. We edged closer together – it was like two strangers coming together for the first time – tentative and uncomfortable. We finally just grabbed each other and held on. We held on for a long time. When we finally did move apart, I tried to come up with something light, something fun to say. I couldn't think of anything except, 'I'm sorry.' Victoria started to speak but I put a finger to her lips. 'I'm sorry I didn't tell you what I was doing. I'm sorry I couldn't let you know more, but he had to be stopped. He was a killer. He needed to kill to live.' That was the truth, anyway.

'And only you could help catch him?'

'But it's done now. He can't hurt anyone now. He's dead.'

'Did she kill him?' The question took me by surprise. There was no lead in to it. No warning that it was coming. The expression on Victoria's face told me that she wanted the truth. It also told me that she was never going to trust Rebecca, no matter what I told her. She wanted to hate Rebecca for the danger she'd got me into – and for the fact that I'd been prepared to take the risks to help Rebecca, come to that. And she was going to do it. What would she think of me if I told her the truth?

'Yes,' I answered. 'She killed him.' I took a deep breath and charged on. 'And I helped her do it.' I had to hold Victoria to stop her from stepping away from me. 'He wasn't a regular serial killer, Victoria. He'd killed hundreds of people. Kept it under the radar. If we hadn't stopped him he would have gone on killing. He enjoyed it. The way things turned out, it was him or us. He would have killed her and he'd have killed me. I didn't enjoy it. I didn't want to do it, but there wasn't an option.'

Victoria didn't say anything. I dropped my hands from her arms and let her go. 'Look, this isn't what you expected. Maybe I should go back to the apartment for now.'

'No!' Victoria caught me before I had managed a step. 'You wouldn't have killed him if you'd had any alternative. I know you.'

A long pause. 'So now what?'

'I don't want to know what happened in New Orleans but if you want to tell me I'll listen. I just need to know that it's finished.'

'It's finished,' I promised. 'Now I just want us to get on with our lives.' I felt like I was pleading with her to let me put this in the past.

'Okay,' she nodded. And then she kissed me. Not a great, passionate kiss, or an erotic one either but I'm sure there was more love in that one kiss than any I can remember us sharing before then.

Victoria took a deep breath – always a sign that she had made her mind up to something. 'You start unpacking and I'll cook us some dinner – unless you'd rather cook while I unpack.'

She'd picked practicality. We would do something constructive and push my trip to New Orleans aside that way. That was fine by me. 'I've had my own cooking for a year,' I said. 'I'll unpack.'

Victoria headed for the kitchen. 'Okay,' she called back. 'And take your jacket off. You're staying.'

I took my jacket off.

Officially, I was on sick leave, so I had some time off and I spent the next three days unpacking my stuff from its boxes. Victoria called in sick the first day but she had to go in to the office for the next two days. That was okay. It gave me the chance to get the feel of the place again. I did normal things. I cooked, tidied the house, got the den the way I like it – just regular stuff, and it felt good to do it. A few of the neighbours were surprised to see me back, but they were pretty friendly. I'd always got on well with them. I just tried to live through some normal days.

And I tried hard not to think of vampires.

We were in bed, late on Thursday night. I was just dozing when Victoria sat bolt upright. 'Shit!'

I fumbled blearily for the bedside light. 'What is it?'

'I'm an idiot!' Victoria fell back to the bed with a groan. 'I booked us for five days in Mexico. We fly on Saturday. I completely forgot about it.'

'How can you forget about booking a vacation?' I asked.

'It's easy,' she snapped. 'When your husband books himself out of hospital and goes God knows where without letting you know.'

There wasn't much arguing with that. I pulled Victoria to me – the first time we'd touched in bed since I came back. 'So we have a vacation in Mexico. Can you think of two people who could use a vacation more than us?'

Victoria wriggled about some, then settled with her head on my chest and shoulder. It felt good. 'I guess not,' she said. 'But I'd have liked longer to get ready.'

I shrugged. 'So tomorrow I pack while you're at work.'

'Mmm,' she purred. 'A personal servant at home. I could get used to that.'

'You haven't seen what I'm going to pack yet,' I answered. 'Two bikinis and that's your lot.'

'Pig.' Victoria said, but she was laughing when she spoke. 'Besides, what makes you think I'll need any clothes at all?' She kissed my chest then added, 'Stud.'

'Are you teasing me, woman?'

'Maybe. Or maybe promising. Time will tell. Goodnight.'

I'd missed that – the closeness with Victoria; the comfortable way we were together. And if she wasn't teasing me, but making a promise for Mexico, our vacation couldn't roll around quickly enough.

Chapter Ten

Mexico was perfect. The weather was ten degrees hotter than we had a right to expect this late in the year and the skies were cloudless. To make things even better our hotel was half empty. Who takes their vacations in October, right? The only downer had been the journey, which had taken three hours longer than the travel company had promised. We'd been delayed on the tarmac at Dallas for almost an hour and then had to circle Mexico City for another hour while we were slotted into their landing schedule. To cap it off, the bus bringing us along the coast to our hotel had popped a tyre – another hour while that was fixed.

So, on our first night, instead of the great, romantic evening I had planned for us, we toppled straight into bed, exhausted and slept for nine hours solid.

The next day was better. We had a late breakfast and sat by the pool in the morning and then wandered around a local market in the afternoon, picking up souvenirs and presents for people at home. We had dinner at the hotel, on a terrace that led directly onto the beach. After dinner, we walked on the beach. Back in our hotel room, we made love. It was the first time we'd had sex in... what? It must have been sixteen months, but it just felt so right. There weren't any great surprises, just a warm sense of belonging. That's the thing about being with someone long-term. You learn how they like to be touched; what gives them pleasure. You tune in to what they want and what they like and the sex gets better. That's how I felt with Victoria.

The next day started pretty well, too. We made love again in the morning and found that we'd missed breakfast. It didn't matter. It was already hot, so we commandeered the best loungers by the pool. I fixed the back so that I'd be sitting upright and then stretched into mine. Victoria thought for a moment then joined me. She pashed my knees apart and sat on my lounger, her back pressed against my chest. She took my arms and wrapped them round her.

'I didn't get much sleep last night,' she said blandly. 'Wake me in an hour.'

A few minutes later, Victoria's head lolled a little and came to rest against my chin. Her breathing was deep and even. A nap seemed like a pretty reasonable idea to me. We were getting some odd looks from other hotel guests but who cared? We were happy.

I settled back and closed my eyes.

It hit me hard, like a wave of energy pinning me to the lounger. I tried to struggle against it but I couldn't move. My brain seemed to be disconnected from my body. I didn't even know if I was still breathing.

Mexico – the hotel, the beach, the sea – it all disappeared. I could still feel Victoria pressed against me, but now I was somewhere else as well. There was an explosion and cold mud rained down on me. Another blast sent me reeling into the deep puddle of mud. All around me, the ground was churned mud. Barbed wire was strewn across the field ahead of me a long deep gouge ran as far as I could see in either direction, disappearing into fog. No, not fog. Smoke. Dead bodies lay all around me. Soldiers – in uniforms from World War One. More shells detonated in the distance, shaking the ground even from miles away. Behind me, someone blew a whistle. A second later, another whistle blew, then another. Soldiers, weary and caked with mud hauled themselves out of the trench and walked slowly in a line towards the enemy. Almost immediately, gunfire came from the German trenches. Half a dozen British soldiers dropped to the mud within seconds. The back of one soldier's head exploded in a burst of crimson and he was thrown backwards into the mud. What sort of tactic was this? World War One. I was in World War One. The Somme, maybe? Or Ypres.

I caught a flash of red out of the corner of my eye. I briefly thought it was another explosion. When I turned, I saw a woman, wearing an ankle length red gown moving across the battlefield. The carnage all around her barely seemed to register with her and even though the battlefield was ankle-deep in mud, her dress was pristine. Any mud or dirt or blood that flew near her seemed to arc away as she moved through the battlefield. No, not through it – she was walking a few inches over it, walking above the ground.

She passed by most of the soldiers. The only time she showed any interest was when a sergeant dropped to his knees, clutching his throat. Blood seeped between his fingers. He choked, gasping for breath and blood frothed out of his mouth. I swear, she laughed at him as he fell into the mud. She was stunning. A perfect figure with long auburn hair framing a stunning face – high cheekbones, a delicate chin, a wide, expressive mouth... but the beauty didn't matter. The expression her face as she watched that sergeant die? It was worse than anything I saw with the vampires. She enjoyed watching the sergeant die. Can a face be brought alive by watching death? She revelled in seeing that man die. She looked all round the battlefield and started smiling at the carnage. People were dying all around her and she loved it. I swear, that beautiful face was the ugliest thing I had ever seen.

Only one soldier could see her. His face was turned away from me but I could see that he was as filthy and tired as his comrades, but when he spoke, he had the calmest voice and I could hear him clearly even through the battle. 'Why here?' he asked the woman.

'It's wonderful, isn't it?' she answered, swinging an arm, as if he needed to have the battle pointed out to him. 'The Somme. The most barbaric battle of a long, brutal war. Men died in their tens of thousands and for what? A few metres of mud?' She paused. 'Nothing to say?'

The soldier's gaze lingered on the battlefield. 'The battle that's coming between us doesn't have to happen.'

'Of course it does,' the woman snapped. 'You've always known it would. The time is coming when the whole world will be like this – chaos and carnage.'

He looked her in the eye, and for the first time she seemed uncomfortable. 'You can stop it,' he said quietly.

'Why would I want to stop it? This will be my world.'

'Once, you offered me the world if I bowed down before you.'

The woman spoke quickly. 'And you refused, fool.'

'Stop our battle before it begins,' he wasn't pleading. He would never plead to her. I knew who they were. I didn't want to accept it. Not even in a dream. He held out his hand to the woman and I tried to turn away or close my eyes. Anything to not see the wounds in his wrists. But I couldn't move and I saw them clearly. Marks where nails had been driven through the wrists when he was crucified. 'Come with me,' he said softly to the woman. 'Take my hand and let go of your hatred and rage. Let me help you set yourself free.'

The woman – no, that was just a front, a façade. I knew who that was, what it really was. It was confused. Surprised, too. 'You're offering me redemption?'

The outstretched hand hadn't wavered. 'Redemption is possible for everyone – even the greatest of sinners. No sin is unforgivable. Take my hand and set yourself free.'

This wasn't like any of the other dreams. They had been linked to Corsini. This was different. Maybe it was a real dream? A genuine nightmare. This couldn't be real. I couldn't be here. And the two people – people? Creatures? Beings?

Myths? The two beings in front of me couldn't be talking like this – because I didn't believe in either of them. But I hadn't believed in vampires either. The rational part of my brain still didn't. How could it accept this meeting between the embodiments of good and evil?

'I... I...' The woman – Devil – whatever you want to call her, stammered. Her eyes were almost glazed over. She couldn't believe the offer being made. She raised her hand, reaching out to the muddied soldier. It was kind of like that Michaelangelo painting. Their fingers brushed...

...and she moved like lightning, slapping his hand away, her face splitting into a snarl. She looked more like an animal than a human being. 'You're afraid!' she spat. 'You know you can't defeat me. Long ago when you cast me out of your miserable utopia, you thought I would shrivel and die. But I survived and I grew stronger.' She was circling the soldier now, like a big cat stalking its wounded prey. Look around you. This isn't your world any more. They're killing each other by the thousand. They don't see the faces of the people they're killing, or know their names. It's chaos and it's anarchy. This is my world now. The people don't listen to you. They've abandoned you. They don't care about anything but themselves. They belong to me now.'

'I set them free,' He answered. 'They belong to no-one but themselves.'

'Set them free? Free to do what? Follow you or be destroyed?'

'Free to choose between right and wrong.' The first time His voice had been raised at all.

'You over-estimate them,' she sneered. 'They are no further forward than they were two thousand years ago. They killed you then. Now...' she paused and cut off a laugh. 'Now you just don't matter to them.'

'You underestimate them. They will never submit to you.'

She tilted her head and stared into his eyes. No fear, only hate. 'They will follow me or I will destroy them. I will destroy them, their world and the I will destroy you.' She moved her face close to His. A little piece of spittle flew from her mouth as she spoke. He didn't flinch as it hit Him. 'Your time is passed Nazarene. And then all of this will be mine, as it should have been so long ago.'

'You cannot win,' he said softly.

'The battle has already begun,' she spun away and stared out and around at the battlefield, drinking in the carnage around her. 'There will be blood, death and despair. It will be glorious.'

The soldier turned and walked slowly away through the mud, carefully picking His way over dead bodies. He looked back at the woman. 'You have already lost.'

He walked away, fog and smoke swirling around him. Before he disappeared, he turned and looked at me – straight at me, and for the first time I saw His eyes. So blue they almost shone. They were filled with compassion but there was determination there, too. And like Rebecca's, those eyes held so much sadness. He nodded to me once and then He turned and was swallowed by the clouds. I turned to look for the woman...

...and sat bolt upright in the lounger. Victoria had to catch at my arm to stop herself being pitched onto the floor. 'Tom?' she yelped. 'What are you playing at?' She turned, pulling back her hand to slap at me. It clicked that she thought I was playing some kind of game. But then she saw my face. She's told me that I was pale but still sweating and that I was shaking uncontrollably.

'Tom? What is it?' Victoria cupped my face. 'What's wrong? I was breathing heavily. It was just a dream. It had to be just a dream. But the way He'd looked at me...

'Tom?' Victoria was worried now. No, scared.

'Nothing!' was about as much as I could choke out.

An arched eyebrow told me Victoria wasn't buying it. I shook my head. 'A bad dream, that's all.'

She flipped stray strands of hair from my eyes and stroked my cheek. 'Still? I thought you were past those.'

'So did I.' My hands were shaking so badly I had to wring them together to keep them under control. I knew what I'd seen. I knew who I'd seen. A dream. It had to be just a dream.

'Was it about her?' Victoria asked. 'In New Orleans.'

I couldn't tell Victoria what I'd seen. I didn't want to tell myself. He'd looked at me. It was a dream. Just a dream. Another fucking dream. Victoria was still waiting for an answer. 'Kind of,' I answered shakily. 'I think it's linked to that.'

Victoria pulled me close. 'It's alright,' she murmured against my neck. 'It's over. It's finished now.'

I wanted to believe her. I told myself over and over that it was a dream. On some superficial level I managed to convince myself that it was my mind playing tricks, picking up on things Rebecca had said.

But that was bullshit.

The dream was real. I had been forced to watch it happen. Forced to know it wasn't over. No matter how hard I tried to deny it, deep inside I knew I had no choice.

While Victoria talked about what we would do when we got back to Dallas, I suddenly realised that I had reached for my phone. I didn't remember doing it, but I was staring at a name and a number.

Rebecca's number.

She had put it in the phone's memory at New Orleans airport. She had known I would call her at some point.

It wasn't over.

BAD BLOOD

BAD BLOOD

BAD BLOOD

COMING SOON

BAD BLOOD
VOLUME TWO
REBECCA

When a dark shroud covers the Earth, a maid shall come, so pure that she casts no shadow and she shall lead the battle into the light.

A girl arrives in 17th century Rome, sent from her village to work for a wealthy merchant's family… and destined to die in his house.

Three centuries later she explores her past and how it affects the gathering of the vampires all across the world.

COMING SOON

BAD BLOOD
VOLUME THREE
GEORGE FISK

A soldier lost among the trenches and barbed wire of a First World War battlefield is found by an enemy far worse than the Kaiser's troops.

A hundred years later he is a soldier in a different army, fighting against vampires and fighting to protect Rebecca and Thomas Lees from the Undead.

BAD BLOOD

In the Twenty-First Century, Vampires are emerging from the shadows. Their attacks are becoming more brazen and public. They are coming together, moving against humanity.

The fate of humanity lies in the hands of a small group of men, women and vampires who have turned their backs on their primal urges and sought redemption.

The epic story of the vampires, from the first of their kind to the last, told in a series of twelve novellas.

VAMPIRES ARE REAL
BELIEVE IT

ERIMEM

THE LAST PHARAOH

by Iain McLaughlin and Claire Bartlett
Foreword by Caroline Morris

After a freak electrical storm that seems to happen indoors, a young woman is found in the Egyptian exhibit of a London museum, and she seems to look exactly like the face on the death-mask of the uncrowned Pharaoh Erimem…

What is she doing inside the exhibit? How did she get there? Is she really a Pharaoh from 1400BC? And just who is willing to search time and space to find and assassinate her?

THE LAST PHARAOH is the first in a series of novels, novellas and short story anthologies taking Erimem, a former companion of the 5th Doctor, on a new set of adventures travelling to the past, the future and into deep space.

THE LAST PHARAOH takes Erimem and a group of 21st century students far into the past, to Actium in Greece where Erimem meets the famed Cleopatra VII on the eve of a vital battle which could end Egypt's existence as a free country and condemn it to life as a Roman province. Two great rulers of Egypt come into conflict over what Egypt needs to do in order to survive, and both Erimem and Cleopatra face their own personal battles for survival.

**Available now from
THEBES PUBLISHING**

ERIMEM

THE BEAST OF STALINGRAD

by Iain McLaughlin

Looking at her timeline, Erimem is intrigued by evidence that at some point in her life, she visits the Nazi-besieged city of Stalingrad in 1942. Against the advice of her friends, Erimem travels back through time to discover what happened in Russia during those terrible times in the war.

Erimem's friends all have the same question - why is she suddenly so obsessed with visiting Stalingrad at this most brutal time?

With German forces relentlessly bombarding the city, the people are freezing and starving... and worse, there are stories of a demon or a beast, stalking the ruined streets of Stalingrad, devouring anyone it meets.

When Erimem arrives she finds a city under attack both from the invading German armies and from a dark force in the shadows..

Also contains THE ONE PLACE, a bonus short story by Claire Bartlett.

BAD BLOOD

.

www.ingramcontent.com/pod-product-compliance
Lightning Source LLC
Chambersburg PA
CBHW070503130626
46555CB00003B/1141